Boy, oh... to do with Alec for the night?

"I'm going to slip into something more comfortable, as they say." Lacey gave a token toss of her hair before slamming the bedroom door on Alec. A confused mix of emotional and physical needs was pinwheeling inside her, but there was nothing she could—or *should*—do about her impulses. Alec obviously didn't want to cooperate. "Well, shoot," she whispered. She almost always got what she wanted...and she wanted him.

Now here they were, two people meant for each other except for the problem of their two wills that would never mesh, not to mention her big mouth and his steely intention to keep his distance.

She turned on the lights and began to squirm out of her spandex miniskirt. Surely then she'd be able to breathe normally. Even with Alec Danieli in the vicinity.

Grandma Lacey-Beth had been wrong. If the devil was in your hand he was already way too close. *One door away. All night long. Sharing pajamas, pillows, toothpaste, kisses...*

Well, maybe familiarity would breed contempt. Though Grandma Lacey-Beth had always said, with a cackle and a wink, "Sweetie-pie, familiarity just breeds."

Dear Reader,

Credit (or should I say *blame*) for this story goes to my editor at Harlequin, Susan Sheppard. I hadn't thought of continuing the erotic adventures begun in my July Temptation, *Black Velvet,* until she suggested that Lacey Longwood—the flamboyant blond bombshell otherwise known as Madame X—simply had to have her own BLAZE book....

And who better to ignite Lacey's BLAZE than bodyguard Alec Danieli, a dark, intense, simmeringly sexy ex-marine with good reason to distrust the notorious "Black Velvet Vixen." To tempt you further, I've mixed in a velvet thong, an obsessed fan, a jealous dog and a dish of hot fudge sauce.

Please help yourself to another serving of sinfully sweet *Black Velvet* fantasy.

Happy reading,

Carrie Alexander

P.S. Look for the third book in this series, *Black Velvet Valentines,* a February '99 Temptation BLAZE title.

Books by Carrie Alexander

HARLEQUIN TEMPTATION
536—FANCY-FREE
598—ALL SHOOK UP
689—BLACK VELVET

HARLEQUIN LOVE & LAUGHTER
8—THE MADCAP HEIRESS
28—THE AMOROUS HEIRESS

A TOUCH OF BLACK VELVET
Carrie Alexander

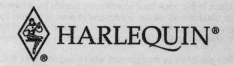

TORONTO • NEW YORK • LONDON
AMSTERDAM • PARIS • SYDNEY • HAMBURG
STOCKHOLM • ATHENS • TOKYO • MILAN • MADRID
PRAGUE • WARSAW • BUDAPEST • AUCKLAND

ISBN 0-373-25804-6

A TOUCH OF BLACK VELVET

Copyright © 1998 by Carrie Antilla.

Printed in U.S.A.

1

He had watched the young woman for a long time now, and he had come to the conclusion that she was a vixen, in all meanings of the word.

Yes, there was something of the wild fox about her—albeit in a rich, sleek, self-satisfied way. The glossy red sheen of her hair made a bewitching contrast to her pale face and black velvet hat and muff. Her eyes were vigilant, her expressions sly, her face triangular, narrowing from its wide brow to a chin as sharp as her voice could be.

Because of her cosseted life-style, she was spoiled, stubborn, demanding.

Despite her cosseted life-style, she had remained untamed.

Until now.

"MADAME X, over here!" called the small group of photographers. "Madame X! Look this way!"

Lacey Longwood torqued her body toward their cameras without shifting her feet. Her dazzling glamour-girl smile was automatic, even when inwardly she was regretting the blinis she'd consumed during lunch at Tavern on the Green with Amalie Dove and her publishers. She slanted her hips to minimize their span, knowing the pose looked sultry rather than self-conscious. Just another of the tidbits she'd picked up from the stick-thin swimsuit girls at her last modeling agency.

Why, oh, why had she allowed that first delicious bite past her lips when she knew this afternoon she'd be the window dressing at another book-signing event, wearing a merciless stretch-black-velvet sheath that showed every sliver of weight gain?

Lacey sucked in her stomach and kept smiling into the glare of the flashing cameras. Because she intended to enjoy every moment of her celebrity, that's why. Even the caloric ones.

She couldn't count on this ever happening to her again. Already her role as Madame X, the spokeswoman for the *Black Velvet* books of erotic short stories, had lasted longer than she'd dared hope. When she'd been asked by her good friend Amalie Dove to assume the identity of the previously anonymous Madame X in Amalie's stead, the gig was supposed to be a top secret, short-term prospect—just two weeks of a book tour and then a discreet fade-out. They hadn't figured on their charade being exposed on the front cover of *NewsProfile*, nor subsequently countless other newspapers and magazines.

But now that it had, Lacey could see no reason not to parlay her *Black Velvet* fame into a few really good modeling and acting jobs as a launchpad for her solo career.

She'd already made two crucial moves. Most important had been dropping her do-nothing agent for the high-powered management team at Piper Hicks, Inc. Piper Hicks had, in turn, landed Lacey a short but promising gig as a featured player on the number one soap opera, *All That Glitters*.

At the thought of her burgeoning career, Lacey

smiled hugely at the photographers. It was real. It was happening. She was finally on her way to the top!

Someone from Pebblepond Press handed her a copy of the first *Black Velvet* story collection, the edition with the notoriously sexy John Singer Sargent painting called *Madame X* on the front. Lacey positioned the book at waist level to show off both the cover and her figure. After all these months as Madame X, she was more than familiar with the photographers' constant refrain: "Don't block the cleavage!"

As it happened, Madame X was *all* cleavage, blond hair and slinky black velvet. Although Lacey had begun playing the part as a whimsical favor to Amalie, becoming famous as Madame X had turned out to be her big break. She couldn't complain about typecasting. Eventually she'd get a chance to display her talent, too.

The fans applauded as Amalie Dove stepped up beside Lacey on the podium. The publicist from Pebblepond Press thrust a copy of the new book, *Black Velvet II*, into the reticent author's trembling hands.

"Smile," Lacey said between her teeth so that her own smile wouldn't dim even one watt. She put a friendly hand on Amalie's shoulders and squeezed reassuringly, tilting her head so the paparazzi could frame both of them in their shots. Amalie blinked at the flashes, something Lacey tried never to do because she didn't want the photographers to catch her with her eyes shut.

"I hate being a spectacle," Amalie murmured, moving her pale lips like an amateur ventriloquist. While she'd finally owned up to being the real author of the racy *Black Velvet* books, she still couldn't bring herself to appreciate the *public* part of public appearances.

"And ever since you started receiving those terrible letters…"

Lacey's Marilyn Monroe smile froze. She didn't want to talk—or even think—about her anonymous "fan" letters, but she didn't want Amalie to be frightened, either. "The notes are meaningless," she said airily. "Even Jericho says it's not likely we're in any danger." *Though grudgingly.* "And the photographers will finish soon enough," she soothed.

Frankly, nuisance notes notwithstanding, she had a hard time understanding Amalie's aversion to publicity. Lacey had been born to the camera, as attested by the thick binders of her mother's meticulously kept photo albums. According to Tricia Longwood, her beautiful baby girl had craved the limelight ever since being named the winner of the toddler division of the Little Miss Magnolia of South Carolina contest.

Amalie shifted her feet nervously. "I'm worried that we look like the Before and After illustrations of a makeover article."

With a sultry dip of her extravagant fake lashes, Lacey glanced down at the shorter woman and whispered, "More like a demonstration of complete opposites."

Amalie was small; Lacey was listed at five-eleven in her modeling portfolio because she'd fudged up a quarter inch—the first time in her life she'd wanted to seem *taller.* Amalie's short, dark hair was fashioned in a feathery pixie cut; Lacey's long, shiny waves were honey gold, with the sunny highlights she'd requested from Arturo, the big-name hairdresser who'd become available only after her sudden celebrity. Amalie was slender, dressed in pale pink; Lacey was perfectly shaped by normal standards but getting too voluptuous for modeling, and of course the fans would be disappointed if she hadn't worn one of her traditional black velvet numbers. Finally, Amalie was shy, gentle and quiet; Lacey was not.

Definitely not.

Lacey Longwood, for the time being best known as the flagrantly sexy Madame X, believed in living large.

And not even the nagging worry of the anonymous, threatening letters could change that!

EXCEPT FOR HER STYLISH showbiz sunglasses, the tiny ninety-pound older woman keeping a careful watch on Madame X from the edge of the crowd didn't look like an agent. Perhaps because Piper Hicks had fallen into the career by happenstance back in the early seventies, when a brain-dead divorce judge had misinterpreted the message of women's lib to mean that a forty-year-old woman who'd sacrificed her youth and beauty to put her husband through medical school and raise his three spoiled children should be perfectly willing to surrender her standard of living and a five-bedroom house in Scarsdale in the name of equality. The minuscule stipend of her alimony had felt more like inequity to Piper, but she'd stiffened her spine, packed her grandmother's pearls and a wardrobe of timeless Chanel suits and found a secretarial position at a New York talent agency. By the time judges had seen the light and were awarding discarded wives half the value of their husband's medical degrees, the talent roster of Piper Hicks, Inc. boasted some of the biggest names in the business.

Since turning sixty-six—she admitted to fifty—Piper had scaled back her involvement in the agency. However, she did like to keep her hand in when an interesting prospect arrived. Despite her own stiff-upper-class WASP upbringing, Piper had taken an unlikely shine to the brash blonde who'd shown up at the office some weeks ago demanding to speak to the boss. While the skintight black velvet ensemble was a bit flashy for Piper's tastes, she'd immediately seen that this over-the-top Madame X creature was bursting with potential. And Piper had a wicked, dead-on eye when it came to spotting potential.

She'd decided to launch Lacey Longwood's career personally. One found so few challenges these days.

Her first order of business had been to take care of Lacey's pesky former agent, Cooper Bennett. Or Bennett Cooper; Piper could never quite recall. Whatever the name, an agent who thought he could do nothing and still collect his percentage was merely roadkill to the legal eagles of Piper Hicks, Inc.

Her second order of business had been to sign Lacey to a lucrative personal-appearance contract with Pebblepond Press. The publishers had been savvy enough to milk the Madame X gimmick for all the publicity they could—which was a lot in the usually stodgy world of literary promotion—but they were paying Lacey peanuts. Piper took care of *that* little annoyance in a couple of phone calls.

Next, in her patented polite but steely way, Piper had wangled an audition with the people at the daytime series *All That Glitters.* She'd decided that a high visibility appearance on the best soap going was the perfect way to cash in on Lacey's hot streak. Daytime serials had an immediacy that movies and television did not.

After Lacey's reading, the show's producers had fallen all over themselves with eagerness to sign her up. They'd even created a bombshell character expressly for her, and were now making noises about extending the role. Which meant extending the contract—a very good thing in Piper's view. Nothing was as satisfying to her as negotiating from a position of power.

Keeping one eye on Lacey as she worked the crowd and the rabid photographers—the girl was gaudy, but she did have a presence—Piper slipped a thin black cellular phone from her vintage Chanel bag and dialed the producers of *All That Glitters.*

Piper Hicks believed in striking while the flashbulb was hot.

IT WAS RAINING in rural Virginia. The Loblolly Club was all but deserted when Alec Danieli walked inside with an express delivery tucked under his arm. He dropped the envelope on a wooden bench by the doors and, shedding rain droplets, shrugged out of his tweed jacket. He hung it on the empty coatrack. Raking his fingers through his shaggy hair, he paused to scan the Loblolly's dim, cavernous interior in a way that was second nature. Besides the bartender, there were a couple of senior citizens at a table drinking beer and playing cards, and a lone twentyish sad sack staring into a dish of peanuts from the depths of a shadowed booth.

Alec glanced toward the bar. It was standard: rows of well-lit glasses and bottles backed by a long, vertical painting of a plump nude draped in a filmy scarf.

"What'll you have?" the bartender asked, pleased to relieve the boredom of a humdrum day.

Alec's dark brows pinched into a frown as he retrieved the package. "Beer," he said, even though he wasn't here for a drink. Accessing the Loblolly's behind-the-bar television and VCR setup was his mission; a beer might help ease the way. "Anything bottled."

"Whatcha got there?" the bartender asked, pointing his blunt chin at the package Alec laid on the bar.

Alec took a stool. Even after more than a year of living on a remote farm nine miles outside tiny Webster Station, Virginia, he wasn't accustomed to the townspeople's habit of sticking their collective noses in one another's business. While he figured the interest was mainly benign, it was unlikely—given his recent history—that he'd ever be comfortable with the locals' penchant for gossip.

Hell, even his more distant history conspired to make him feel out of place in Webster Station. His father, Franco Danieli, had been in the foreign service; Alec had grown up in embassies around the world. Thus, exotic environments were already his norm when his own career in the military had sent him to even farther flung—and less civilized—outposts. He'd learned to live by his own wit, skill and instinct. And sometimes by the law of the jungle...even when there'd been no jungle in sight.

All of which meant that to Alec Danieli, small-town America was an alien environment.

The bartender was still waiting. "A videotape," Alec finally answered, because it suited him to do so. He up-ended the open envelope and the tape fell out onto the bar with a clatter.

"Madame X?" the bartender said, squinting at the label. "Whozzat?"

Alec drew on his beer. "Damned if I know." Lacking both a TV and a VCR, as well as any interest in the pap they spewed, he simply wasn't up on pop culture. One corner of his mouth curled into a sarcastic grimace. *Man, what a waste.*

The bartender, a middle-aged tough-guy type with a navy anchor insignia tattooed on his hairy forearm, turned the videotape over in hands the size of catcher's mitts. He gestured at the television. "Wanna play it?"

Alec sighed. "Why not," he said, even though there were a thousand reasons why not. But a promise was a promise, and Thomas Janes Jericho, a name from a past that Alec was trying to put behind himself, was calling in his marker.

The videotape was brief. It began with a short news story about two women from South Carolina who were responsible for a couple of books of erotica titled *Black Velvet*, moved on to a talk show host's interview with the blonde calling herself Madame X, and ended with the same woman's appearance on a soap opera, where she played—in a stunning display of creativity—a famous author named "Velvet Valancy," whose only purpose on the show seemed to be to seduce the male half of the cast's young-and-happily-marrieds.

Alec scoffed in disbelief, and drained his beer in a long pull. Jericho had to be kidding.

"Let's watch it again," said the bartender, rewinding.

The two older men abandoned their card game and took the stools on either side of Alec. "G'wan," one of them said eagerly. "Start the tape."

Briefly Alec closed his eyes, straining for objectivity even though the mere sight of the gorgeous blonde had inundated him with memories of a similarly gorgeous blonde who'd monopolized his final, fatal assignment in a tiny speck of a country in the Middle East. Sternly he told himself that except for a dye bottle, there was no connection between the two.

"That's Madame X," said one of the seniors. He leaned past Alec to nudge his buddy. "Remember, Elmer? Mitzi showed us that Madame X book, *Black Velvet* something or other."

"Hot stuff," said Elmer, his rheumy eyes widening

as the larger-than-life blonde cavorted across the screen.

Alec groaned and leaned his head on his hand. Naturally, this "Madame X" was a looker. Regardless of the entirely too obvious come-and-get-me-you-know-I-want-it velvet dress and stiletto heels.

She was also polished and well-spoken, handling the graceless interviewer with cool competence even while the smile she aimed at the camera carried a tangible warmth. Alec frowned when he caught himself wanting to smile back. He'd already learned the hard way that a warm smile and a beautiful face did not an honest woman make.

The scenes from the soap opera were replaying. "This is *All That Glitters*," said the bartender.

Alec shaded his eyes. "I wouldn't know."

"Yeah, yeah," the bartender murmured. "See there, Case and Ashleigh are just back from their honeymoon in Cozumel."

The two old-timers chortled. Realizing he'd been caught out, the sheepish bartender held up his hands. "Hey, whaddya want? So I watch the soaps. There's nothing else to do in this joint during the day."

All three men returned their gazes to the television screen. Alec's had never left. Velvet Valancy was putting the moves on studly Case in a hot tub. She was wearing a black velvet bikini until she peeled the straps down her arms, whereafter she wore only a cloud of steam. The crests of her bountiful breasts dipped into the bubbling water a split second before the camera zoomed in for their close-up. In spite of himself, Alec's libido stirred.

The videotape cut to a shot of a woman screaming as her car plunged off a bridge. The bartender made a sound of frustration. "Rats. I musta missed this episode when the ladies' auxiliary met here last Friday. I sure hope they didn't kill off Ashleigh."

The mopey young man had left his booth to join them. "They didn't," he contributed, almost enthusiastically. "She's in a coma."

While the young man and the bartender discussed the plot ramifications of comas and infidelity, Alec concentrated on willing his body into compliant detachment—which was tougher than it ought to have been. He'd been too long without a woman to dismiss Madame X's racy curves without a lingering mental pit stop. Which was all it was, he promised himself. Nothing but his hormones were involved. And he'd get even those in hand—*Better make that "under control,"* he thought—before too long.

The bartender had neglected to shut off the videotape. After commercials, they were back to the hot tub. Velvet and Case kissed hungrily. "Oh, please," Alec said, making the entreaty sound sarcastic rather than desperate.

Elmer smacked his lips. "Lookee that."

Slowly the camera panned down the twisting, slippery, suggestively nude bodies to hold on a shot of frothing water. The background music reached its pulsing crescendo. A fade to black and a screenful of static signaled the abrupt end of the tape.

"Hoochie mama!" Elmer crowed. "Can we play it again?"

Alec crumpled the delivery envelope in his fist. "It's all yours, men," he said, sliding off the stool. "Go crazy." He took out his wallet and laid a bill on the bar. "And have one on me."

"Heyah, thanks, buddy," said the young man. "Say, aren't you the guy who bought the old McDuffie place way out on Rockridge Road?"

"That's right." Lifting one hand in an otherwise silent goodbye, Alec snagged his jacket off the rack and left without introducing himself. Introductions only led to questions, and questions might lead to disconcerting disclosures. He'd gone the "Don't I recognize you from somewhere?" route a hundred times too often.

"Doesn't say much, does he?" observed one of the seniors after the double doors had banged shut behind Alec.

Elmer snapped the twenty-dollar bill. "Sometimes words ain't necess'ry. Set 'em up, Rob."

The bartender began to draw another round of beers. "Looks kinda familiar. Ex-marine, I'm betting," he mused, referring to Alec, "but all the same he can't be too bad if he tapes *All That Glitters*."

The young man nodded. "He's got good taste."

Elmer smacked his lips again. "I got me a taste for Madame X." He waggled his index finger in a circle. "Let's rewind and watch her again, boys."

IF ONLY THE RAIN could wash me clean....

Alec sat on the brick front steps in the drizzle, staring out at the rolling green hills of his farm as a familiar, bitter anger etched its acid into his heart. He tilted his face up, letting the rainwater that was dripping off the pediment spatter his closed eyelids and run down his cheeks like tears.

Nineteen months ago he'd still been clean....

He cursed. Awhile back he'd promised himself that he wasn't going to dwell on the incident that had ended his career in the marines, promised that he was going to concentrate only on the here and now. Which was a tough enough task even when all connections between his present life and the past had been severed.

Watching the videotape of the familiar-seeming Madame X had made the promise all that more difficult to keep.

Could he withstand a constant proximity to the real-life article without getting eaten up inside by sour self-flagellation?

Raindrops trickled off Alec's chin as he lowered it to stare with flat, mud-brown eyes at the pristine white board fence that set off a verge of grass and the new gravel of the curved driveway. The huge oak at the bend dripped with rain. The yearlings' flanks glistened wetly as they nosed around the paddock. Alec had worked long and hard, running the place pretty much by himself, eschewing many of the creature comforts—like gorgeous blondes who flaunted their magnificent breasts—in a kind of self-imposed exile. And he wasn't yet ready to break his monastic existence.

Certainly not for a woman like Madame X.

But at Jericho's request...

Alec took the crumpled envelope out of his jacket pocket. Although he'd left the videotape back at the Loblolly, the photocopied letters were still inside— three nasty, anonymous letters addressed to Madame X. He reread them, automatically employing his specialized training to gauge the writer's ultimate intent.

Were the notes harmless, simply the creepy but standard ramblings of a nutty fan? Or were they as serious as Jericho had come to believe?

A raindrop plopped onto the paper, running the ink in the phrase "two-faced vixen." The words hit too close to home for Alec; again anger and distrust pierced his objectivity.

He tossed back his head, his mouth open, gulping the cool, fresh air. Nineteen months ago, at an embassy in the Middle East, he'd tangled with a woman very

much like Jericho's Madame X, and look where that
had got him—

No. He refused to think that way.

By all rights, he should be able to take on this pid-
dling assignment with one hand tied behind his back.
Madame X might be a flighty, flashy, dazzling type of
woman, but she was no Mata Hari. And as it had already been irrevocably trashed, this time around his
reputation was not at risk.

Yes, Alec could easily fulfill Jericho's request.

He could be Madame X's bodyguard.

ONCE AMALIE DOVE had been acknowledged as the actual author of the *Black Velvet* books, Lacey had expected to get the big kiss-off from Pebblepond Press—
particularly as she'd been an equal partner in fooling
the publishers into believing that *she* was the author.
Money and publicity spoke louder than scalded pride,
however, and luckily the readers were enamored with
Lacey's characterization of the outrageous Madame X.

Thanks to Piper Hicks, Lacey was now earning a le-
gitimate salary for being the books' "spokesperson."
During the past several months of strong sales, Pebblepond's PR flacks had scheduled her for appearances at
malls and bookstores across the country. Usually solo,
because ever since Amalie's marriage to Thomas Jericho—the journalist who'd uncovered their *Black Velvet*
masquerade—the real author preferred staying put at
home on an island off the South Carolina coast, revel-
ing in newlywed bliss as she worked on her next book.

It was left to Lacey to pose in her slinky black velvet
dresses for photos with fans, pass out stacks of autographed publicity shots and make appearances on talk
shows in her guise as Madame X. At book-signing
events, the readers always insisted that she autograph

their copies even though she was only the author's representative. Attaining Madame X's red lipstick imprint beneath her signature had become a coveted bonus. Lacey signed, laughed, chatted and even occasionally read passages from Amalie's erotic writings. And she smiled until her cheeks hurt.

Celebrity status was everything she'd imagined it would be. She loved it.

She wanted more.

That should be my motto, Lacey thought as the photo op concluded and most of the photographers dispersed. *Like Veruca Salt, the spoiled girl from* Willy Wonka and the Chocolate Factory, *I want more of everything and I want it now.* She remembered watching the movie as a child, knowing that she was supposed to learn a moral from Veruca's fate, and not caring one whit. Already she'd craved the kind of fancy dress, fame and fortune that one didn't find in her dinky rural hometown in South Carolina.

Lacey and Amalie were escorted from the stage and through the crowd, past the table where they would soon be signing books. A scheduled ten-minute break gave Lacey just enough time to freshen her makeup; instead she stopped to watch as Jericho came up to Amalie and put his arm around her protectively. Amalie looked up into his face and smiled, obviously comforted by his presence.

The way they touched each other gave Lacey an unexpected twinge. Although she'd enjoyed an intense flirtation with the action movie star Lars Torberg during her initial tour as Madame X, and had acquired a large number of admirers since, there was presently no special man in her life. And she'd *never* experienced the kind of love that radiated from Jericho and Amalie, brighter than the biggest klieg light Hollywood had to offer.

Preferring to concentrate on what she had instead of what she lacked, Lacey brushed aside her discontent to focus on the thrill of her celebrity. Exchanging a quick wave with Amalie and Jericho, she went to find Piper Hicks.

The sight of the agent in her suave sunglasses and black-and-gray, houndstooth-check Chanel suit gave Lacey goose bumps. Even though her previous agent had talked a smooth game, Lacey had soon realized that he'd been more interested in making a quick buck off her sudden fame than in helping her develop a lasting career.

Piper Hicks was the complete opposite. She had true class. She was big-time. And she could send Lacey's career into the stratosphere.

Lacey hurried over to the agent. "Mrs. Hicks, I really appreciate your showing up. My last agent couldn't seem to detach his ear from his cell phone or hoist his butt out of his desk chair to save his life."

The supercilious arch of the agent's penciled brows made Lacey realize how inelegant she'd sounded. She stifled a nervous laugh in response, keenly aware of the importance of maintaining her glamorous image. Although she'd tried to polish her small-town beauty queen naiveté into a slick city sophistication, frequently her natural enthusiasm revealed itself. She'd just never be a truly blasé Manhattanite.

Still, in the face of Piper's well-bred reserve, Lacey did her best to chill out. She cranked down the wattage of her smile, trying instead to emulate the cool elegance of Grace Kelly in *Rear Window*. That should do the trick.

Piper rewarded her with a small nod. "I like to keep

track of the talent, Lacey. And do call me Piper. I'm too old and decrepit to stand on ceremony."

Hah! "Well, really, I—" Lacey swallowed "—I certainly don't think of you as old, Mrs—Piper. But you are an icon." She smoothed her palms down her velvet-clad hips. *Oh, what the heck.* "This will probably sound like gushing, but I've got to say that I've been counting my lucky stars since the day you signed me up as a client."

"How sweet." Piper removed her sunglasses, letting them dangle on a pearl-studded chain. Her small green eyes were deep set, rimmed with sallow circles and crepey skin. She was nimble, trim and energetic, though, with a puffy halo of striking auburn hair and a take-charge attitude that firmed her soft mouth and delicate features.

"I've been negotiating with the producers of *All That Glitters,*" she said. "You'll be happy to know that I believe we have a deal."

"They're serious about keeping me on? We have a deal?" Lacey jittered in place, barely managing to squelch her squeal of excitement. She did take Piper's hands and kiss her rouged cheek, actually wanting to grab the tiny agent up in a bear hug but afraid of crushing the older woman's fragile bones in her excess of enthusiasm. Lacey poured the overflow into her rich contralto voice. "Oh, thank you, Mrs. Hicks, thank you. Thank you so much."

Piper smiled and patted Lacey's hands. "We haven't signed the new contract quite yet, my dear. And judging by today's turnout, they'll be lucky to get you when we do. Keep that in mind."

Lacey's eyes gleamed. "Oh, gosh, I'm a professional actress! After all these years I can't believe it's happened."

Piper emitted a dry chuckle. "Believe it, Lacey. You're on your way."

"I promise you I'll do everything I can to fulfill your expectations. I want more than anything to be a success." Lacey ignored another small twinge of misgiving produced by the thought of the anonymous letters. "Anything," she repeated staunchly.

Piper's sculpted nose twitched as she opened her black leather bag and took out a pair of chamois driving gloves. "There's the attitude I like. If my clients didn't have it, they wouldn't be my clients." Her tone was precise, the challenge implicit. The Piper Hicks talent agency didn't demand excellence and loyalty—it expected it as a matter of course.

"Here's your escort," Piper said, flapping her gloves at the approach of a well-built young man in a khaki security-guard uniform.

"My escort," Lacey echoed faintly, falling from her high with a nearly audible thud. Because she was an independent sort, the need for security details and bodyguards was one part of fame that would take some getting used to.

In light of the threatening letters, Piper had exchanged a discreet word with bookstore personnel about Madame X's overeager fans. As a result, mall cops were swarming today's event. To Lacey it seemed like overkill. Then again, she couldn't help but be flattered that she—and Amalie, too—were considered such precious and important personages.

She turned to the mall's security guard, giving him her best Marilyn Monroe flutter-wink-smile-and-coo. He melted in his boots, turning red and stammering, "The-they're waiting, Miss, uh, Ms. Madame X."

"I'll be in touch with the details of the new contract,"

Piper said, drawing on her gloves finger by finger. "Till then, continue as before, Madame X."

As the agent walked away to a rendezvous with her chauffeur-driven limo, Lacey drew a deep breath and tossed her head, defiantly flicking a lock of her lustrous golden hair over one shoulder. Leaving college a semester short of graduation and subsequently surviving six long years of struggling to establish herself as an actress in the competitive jungle of Manhattan had proved that she was up to any challenge. A few poison pen letters would not spoil her enjoyment of this much-anticipated success.

She took the arm of the security guard and let him lead her to the table where Amalie had already been seated. Jericho hovered behind his wife with his hands on her shoulders. His pale green eyes scanned the crowd, looking for trouble. Lacey hesitated, then shook her head, still refusing to let a few measly threats dampen her enthusiasm.

The jostling queue of fans applauded at her arrival. She paused to wave and blow kisses before sashaying over to take her place beside Amalie. Everything was A-okay. Peachy keen. She couldn't ask for more.

Stacks of books had been piled on the left side of the table, nearest to Lacey. As the bookstore employees unsnapped the velvet rope that had been holding back the crowd, Lacey took down the first copy of *Black Velvet II*. Its velveteen cover slipped through her fingers and the book dropped facedown on the table, pages splayed.

"Whoopsy-daisy," Lacey said, hoping she hadn't creased any of the corners, or Amalie—a book-loving librarian—would have her head. Lacey righted the volume and quickly riffled through it.

An icy hand closed around her heart. *"Jericho,"* she said in an urgent whisper.

Both he and Amalie tensed at the tightness in Lacey's voice. Even though the menacing letters had been addressed to Madame X and delivered to Lacey along with her fan mail, all three of them had been affected by the vile insults and nasty threats.

"Is there a problem?" Jericho asked quietly, bending his tawny head toward Lacey. His arm looped around Amalie's shoulders, pulling her in closer.

Lacey held the book open so they could see what was inside.

Amalie gasped.

Jericho straightened and waved a couple of the store's security guards over to the table. The crowd stirred in puzzlement, buzzing with rising curiosity.

The bookstore manager elbowed his way past the security guards. "What's the delay?"

Jericho was pulling books off the stack, flipping them open one by one and tossing them aside. Amalie exchanged stricken glances with Lacey, her dark blue eyes wordlessly revealing her devastation.

"It's my secret admirer," Lacey said woodenly, even though the absurdity of the expression suddenly seemed hysterically incongruous. Her *admirer!*

She picked up several of the discarded books and opened them to the defaced pages. On book after book, page after page, one word had been inked over and over again in crude, sprawling, bloodred letters:

Vixen

2

He was her chauffeur and pseudo bodyguard, but he didn't act like an employee. Laryssa hadn't yet made up her mind how she felt about that....

She eyed him petulantly from beneath the rolled velvet brim of her hat. "Daniels! Snap to it, man. Bring my parcels inside at once—up to my bedroom. I want to look over my purchases before I have to dress for dinner."

Daniels—she still didn't know his first name—whipped shut the door of her father's classic black Rolls and came around to the trunk, the keys held silently in his leather-gloved hand. Daniels was solid and quiet and deliberate—not the jingling-keys type.

The thickening snow had already dusted the shoulders of his camel-hair topcoat. "You sound like a spoiled brat," he said evenly, adding the proper nomenclature as an afterthought: "Miss Laryssa."

Her pouting lips tightened. She could never seem to get a rise out of him—of any kind. "How appropriate, dear Daniels," she snapped, "as it seems I am one."

"You need to be taught a lesson."

Laryssa's eyes lit up. "By whom?" she demanded. A tremor passed through her. Inside the warm velvet muff her fingertips tingled with excitement. "Certainly not you!"

THE PACKAGE WAS WRAPPED in plain brown paper with no return address, and Madame X was being naive enough—or dumb enough—to open it.

Alec burst through the dressing room door and grabbed the parcel out of her hands. "Hey—ouch!" she howled. "You broke one of my nails."

Oh, man, he thought. She *would* be a prima donna.

"Give me that back," she demanded, rising to her full, impressive height so they stood eye-to-eye. She reached for the package.

"Watch the nails," Alec said with dry sarcasm, holding the box on his fingertips out of her reach—just barely. She was a healthy, blooming specimen of womanhood even if she did care more about her manicure than her safety.

"Nails?" Her heavily made up eyes narrowed. "I'll show you nails."

Catching him unaware—all right, he needed a few seconds to adjust to the shockingly vivid reality of her—she went on tiptoe, one elegant hand flashing out to snag the parcel. Alec held on to the other end and they tugged it back and forth between them like two kids with one candy bar.

"Has it occurred to you that this package may have been sent by your anonymous fan?" he asked.

She let go, nine perfect and one imperfect bright red nails flying up so her hands shielded her face. "Then take it away!"

"No need." Alec set the package on her dressing table, placing it on top of an *All That Glitters* script because every square inch of tabletop was filled by the tubes and bottles and jars of her feminine-type clutter.

"It's probably nothing," he said, squatting to examine the underside of the box as he cautiously tilted it up.

"Careful," she warned, backing off with a soft swish of silk.

Alec glanced sideways at her toes. Also painted shiny red, they peeped enticingly from beneath the hem of her peacock blue robe.

"I'm always careful," he said, but an image of a blue-eyed blonde with Tatar cheekbones—from the one time he hadn't been careful enough—passed through his mind's eye. In the next instant he had banished the woman from his thoughts and deliberately returned his attention to the package as though there'd been no distraction at all. "You might try it sometime," he added.

"All right, I will." Out of the corner of his eye, he saw that Madame X had set her hands on her nicely proportioned, flagrantly female hips and was glaring a challenge at him. "Who are you?"

"Not your anonymous fan." *Or a fan of any type*, he reminded himself. *Just a detached surveyor of... proportions.*

She crept up behind him; he could smell the flowers-in-rain scent of her perfume. "I wouldn't call Mr. Anonymous a *fan*, exactly."

Alec wrinkled his nose. "Right." He scratched it. "Where did you get this package?"

She leaned a little closer, bending to stare at the seemingly innocuous box, the ends of her long blond hair sweeping his shoulder and tickling the side of his face. "Someone from the show brought it in with the rest of the fan mail."

Alec moved his shoulders negligently, then leaned forward on the tips of his fingers to study the way the brown paper was folded and taped around the sides of the small parcel. *Concentration.* He was usually good at it.

His two-legged preoccupation inched even closer. "What do you see?"

Alec's gaze dropped to her toes again. They were curling into the plush carpet, the gleaming red nails perplexing because they were so distracting. "Why are you whispering?"

"I don't know," she whispered. "It just seemed like the thing to do."

He stood abruptly, forcing her to back off. "I don't see anything particularly suspicious about this package except for the lack of a return address. Still, it pays to be careful in light of the other incidents."

"I suppose so." She sounded reluctant. "You still haven't told me who you are."

"And see how easily I've made it into your dressing room— a total stranger."

"Y'all aren't..." she slid her hands into the pockets of her shimmery dressing gown and stared at him, eyes so round her irises looked like big blue marbles "...dangerous," she finished in a whisper.

"How do you know?"

With a flick of her lashes, she indicated the telephone near the dressing table. "I can call security—" once again her hand flashed out, but this time she only snapped her fingers "—like that."

To teach her a lesson, Alec stepped in front of the telephone. She surprised him by making a feint toward it and then lunging for the open door. "Guard!" she bellowed, getting halfway into the hall before Alec closed his hand around her wrist.

"I was only testing you," he said into her ear, drawing her back inside. "It's all right."

She must have believed him. She came easily, closing the door by leaning against it, her breasts shifting under the peacock silk as the knob turned and the door thudded shut. With a herculean effort, Alec held his gaze steady on her face. It was a beautiful face, no two ways about it: a bone structure sculpted to perfection; creamy complexion; wide, impossibly blue eyes; glossy lips pouting with promises of decadence....

He clenched his teeth. While Madame X was not a carbon copy of the notorious spy-for-hire Ecaterina "Cat" Szako, she came close enough to raise his hackles. Purposefully, he reminded himself that regardless of physical similarities, this woman did not have Cat's motives. And in any case, he would not be getting emotionally involved in *this* assignment.

A deep breath shuddered in and out of Madame X, doing interesting things to the parts of her he wasn't looking at. "You can let go of me any time you'd like," she said with such a calm assurance he knew she'd fought to maintain it.

He had more reason than she to be frazzled by their proximity. He was hoping that she couldn't tell. "Yes," he agreed, and lifted his hand away. His palm tingled with an awareness that up to now had always meant his sixth sense had kicked in. Maybe it still did.

He went back to the package and resumed studying it, narrowing his focus to shut out all other distractions. "Hand me that...that—" He pointed.

"Emery board," she said, placing it in his hand.

He slid the emery board under the brown paper flap and pried it up.

"Boom," Madame X said into his ear, her husky voice full of unspilled laughter.

He took a deep breath. "Not so funny if this turns out to be a hair-trigger letter bomb."

"Didn't you hear? They caught the Unabomber."

Alec slid a plain white gift box out of the paper wrappings. "It's highly unlikely that Ted Kaczynski's your troublesome Mr. X," he murmured, testing the flimsy weight of the box. He scanned the dressing table, picked up an odd-looking apparatus and worked the tweezerlike handles experimentally. After a quick glance at Madame X in the mirror—she appeared wary but amused—he used the emery board to pry off the top of the gift box and fold back several layers of red tissue paper.

"Aw, c'mon," she said, shrugging off her caution to reach for the box. "I really don't think you need my eyelash curler to snare—"

"There may be fingerprints," Alec explained, even though he was almost certain that the parcel hadn't been mailed by Mr. X. To be one hundred percent safe, he used the apparatus to lift some pitifully besotted fan's idea of a love token from the box. Extending his arm, he slowly turned the strange item in the air.

Dangling from the eyelash curler was what appeared to be an elasticized black velvet pouch strung on a tangle of loops.

"Congratulations." Madame X threw back her head and laughed—a laugh that was so sweet and rich Alec felt it in the marrow of his bones. "You've just rescued me from a pair of men's underwear."

"I don't get it," the uninvited stranger kept saying.

"Well, I'll try to explain it to y'all." Impishly, Lacey plucked the velvet underwear from the eyelash curler. "See, this here's the, umm…pouch." She grinned. "Or the banana hammock, if you prefer. And this part goes behind, so to speak, up between the—"

"I know what a thong is. I was just wondering why some guy you've never met would send one to you."

Seated on her padded silk moiré dressing table chair,

she twirled the skimpy piece of underwear on the tip of her finger. "Same reason women used to throw lingerie at Tom Jones in concert, I expect."

The guy still didn't have a clue. "Appreciation," she elaborated, "and to signal their availability."

He rolled his eyes. "Oh, man…"

"We could read the card."

He looked mildly interested, but when he started to root inside the box with the idiotic eyelash curler, she reached past him. "Honestly," she said, "this isn't a case for Agent 007." Even though this stranger did look a bit like a downscale James Bond in his long, fawn-colored trench coat and the black jeans and turtleneck. But he needed a haircut and shave, and he certainly wasn't trying to be charming.

"'Dearest Madame X,'" she read. "'Please accept my own personal undergarment as proof of my passion.…'"

"Sorry now that you touched them?"

"They're clean," she insisted with a small shudder, and skimmed the rest of the note. "Yikes, listen to this. 'Would you send me a pair of yours, preferably unwashed, by return mail?'" She laughed and flicked the notecard away. "I don't think so!"

Her Bondish visitor claimed the card. "After what happened at the book signing, this is not a laughing matter."

"That was just a vicious prank. No one was hurt." Lacey frowned. *Except Amalie, who loves her books as though they're her children.*

With clouded eyes she stared into the mirror, imagination painting the word *vixen* across her reflection in lurid red letters. She'd been trying not to dwell on the incident, but now and then it got to her. She couldn't help but wonder what she'd done to incite such hostility. Was this just the price of success—or the beginning of a campaign of escalating terror?

"'With all my love...'"

Lacey made a mental effort to sweep away the negative vibes. Long ago she'd learned to be a relentlessly positive thinker—a tactic developed to counteract years of career rejection. "Gosh, thanks," she said brightly.

"'...Brian O. Malcolm,'" her self-appointed protector finished dubiously. He tucked the card into a jeans pocket. "I'll check this out, but it's probably a fake name."

"*You'll* check it out." Lacey swiveled the chair around on its casters so she could stare up at him. "And who'll be checking you out, may I ask?"

Although he moved his lips into a semblance of a smile, his eyes remained somber, giving away nothing as his gaze traveled up and down the length of her. Not caring to seem intimidated by his tough-guy demeanor, she crossed what she knew to be her fabulously long legs, lolling back in the chair as her dressing gown parted to reveal their tanned contours four inches above the knee. Let him look. She'd withstood the most stringent of perusals.

Her visitor cleared his throat. "I guess you could say that Jericho already has."

"You know Thomas Jericho? Amalie's husband?"

"Sort of." His glance dropped to her legs, then bounced back up to her face. His eyes were black and sharp and bright, like chips of polished obsidian.

Only lust could make a man's eyes look like that, Lacey thought. Suddenly nervous in her triumph, she uncrossed her legs. "You're friends with Jericho?"

"Acquaintances, anyway. I owed him a favor."

Forgetting their unspoken battle, Lacey sat forward. "Past tense?" she prodded.

Again her visitor cleared his throat. Now he was looking everywhere but at her. "You're the favor," he admitted.

"Me?" She popped to her feet, drawing the robe tightly closed.

"Yes. Didn't Jericho tell you?"

"Tell me what?"

"I'm Alec Danieli. Your bodyguard."

"JERICHO WANTS TO TALK to you," Lacey said with exasperation, holding out the telephone to the man who had apparently been appointed her brand-new bodyguard whether or not she approved. Alec Danieli took the phone and turned away from her, murmuring into the receiver in a voice so low she couldn't catch everything he said.

Not that she wanted to, Lacey decided, glaring so fiercely at the back of Alec's shaggy head that it should have melted under the heat. Let him and Jericho run around playing their macho little games. It didn't matter to her. She was quite capable of defending herself from renegade black velvet thongs—with or without a bodyguard!

Even before checking with Jericho, she'd remembered that after the "vixen" vandalism, they'd discussed the possibility of getting protection for her and Amalie. The mere *possibility*, was what she'd heard, assuming that it was far from a done deal even though Jericho had mentioned his contact, an ex-marine who had experience with this type of thing.

Lacey had pictured a tall, crude, hulking hunk of testosterone with a salt-and-pepper buzz cut, a bull neck and thin, straight lips. Certainly not a lithe panther of a man who was probably no more than half an inch taller than she; a man with wavy, blue-black hair, a narrow blade of a nose, burning-coal eyes and lips too generous for the rest of his austerely handsome features…lips that were at once so cruel and so sensual they ought to be outlawed.

Nor had she expected a man who'd show up at her dressing room door and try to take over her life.

"A bodyguard," she muttered. *Pah!* What did she need with a bodyguard?

Despite the occasional misgiving, she truly wasn't as worried about the situation as Amalie and Jericho were. In a way the notes were a symbol that she'd arrived. Dealing with obsessive fans was a part of being a celebrity.

The vandalism at the book signing was more disturbing, though. Lacey had to admit that at first it had given her a good case of the heebie-jeebies. But she'd evaluated the situation and decided that the doorman at her apartment building and the guards on the soap opera set and at *Black Velvet* events were all the security she needed. Besides, at almost five-eleven and a robust one hundred and forty some pounds, she was no pushover. One of the first things she'd done when she'd moved to New York was to take a defense class. A couple of years ago she'd even outmuscled a mugger in a tug-of-war for her purse, so it should have been clear to all concerned that she knew how to take care of herself.

Lacey's gaze was drawn to Alec. He stood with his head bent to the telephone, one hand stuck in the pocket of his narrow black jeans, the unbelted trench coat hanging open with casual elegance. Although he wasn't muscle-bound, his body appeared to be honed to a lean, ascetic perfection. The kind of male perfection that made every tiny hair on her body spring to attention.

Well, so what? She could take care of herself...in *any* situation.

Alec hung up the phone. "We're having dinner with Jericho and Amalie at eight."

Lacey drew herself up and swiveled to face the mirrored dressing table. "Are we?" she said archly, spritzing her face with a mist of bottled water. She'd discovered that the hot lights on the set were terribly drying for her skin.

"Yes. To talk over the situation."

Her eyes searched him out in the mirror, pulled unerringly to his face as though he were a hypnotist. "I don't want a bodyguard, you know."

He turned away, so busy visually cataloging the contents of her cluttered dressing room that he didn't bother to respond. Obviously he was one of those frustrating men who don't *listen* even when they've heard. "I don't want a bodyguard," she insisted, raising her voice a notch.

"You don't have to yell. I heard you the first time."

"I don't think you did." Her eyes shot blue flames at his reflection as she carefully reiterated, "I said I do not need a bodyguard."

"That's where you're wrong." His voice was even and unperturbed, his eyes lingering on the silver-blond pageboy wig that the *All That Glitters* costumer had suggested for one of Lacey's scenes as Velvet Valancy. "Do you have any other wigs? Some other color, perhaps?"

She smoothed her hair. "I don't wear wigs."

"You will."

Her smile was tight. "I prefer my hair as it is, thank you."

Alec's glance touched on her gleaming golden head. "So does Mr. X. Didn't one of the notes mention your beautiful blond hair—and how sorry you'd be if something happened to it?"

She shrugged, frowning as he continued to prowl around the dressing room.

"I think it would be a good idea to alter your appearance. Glasses—"

She brightened. "I have a pair of killer sunglasses."

Alec winced. "I had in mind something less Hollywood. Horn-rims, thick lenses, that kind of thing."

"Yechh."

His eyes clashed with hers in the mirror. "The thing is to make you unrecognizable." His gaze dropped to her figure. "There's nothing we can do about your height, but padding would help."

Lacey shot up, one hand pressed between her breasts, defensively clutching the lapels of the peacock robe. "Padding—hah! You've got to be kidding." She worked too hard at the gym maintaining her figure to suffer the ignominy of padding on some make-work bodyguard's say-so. "No way, no how. Forget it, Danieli."

Alec stopped pacing the small room and turned to stare at her. "'Vanity, thy name is Woman.'"

"I am not vain."

He made an accusatory sound, his cruel top lip twitching with an impending sneer.

Nostrils flaring, she tilted her chin at him. "You don't understand. It's not a matter of vanity. I'm a celebrity. My fans expect me to uphold a certain standard. I can't be parading around in gunnysacks and Bozo wigs and—and—*padding*, for Pete's sake!" She whipped the skirt of the robe around, flounced back into the chair and started combing her hair. "I'm telling you, I will not do it."

"Are you willing to pay for your fame with your life?"

The comb stilled for a moment, then swept smoothly through her long hair. "You're overstating the case."

Alec put his hand on the back of her chair and swiveled her around to face him. He squatted on his heels before her. Lacey stared into his eyes, suddenly short of breath as all the muscles in her abdomen contracted at once.

"Maybe," he said. "And maybe not. Are you willing to take the chance?"

She said faintly, "This kind of thing happens...."

"The letters, yes. But the vandalism of the books has stepped up the game." His fingertips brushed across her knuckles, easing open her fingers so he could take the comb from her clenched hand. He stretched to place it on the dressing table, the movement momentarily pressing his hard chest against her kneecaps.

Lacey looked down at her empty hands curled loosely in her lap. They were shaking slightly; Alec kindly took them into his. "How do we even know the two are connected?" she whispered.

"The word that was written in the books," he said, soothing her with his smooth voice, his gentle hands. "Have you heard it from anyone before?"

"Mmm." She felt as though she were sinking into a plush velvet sea, all her worries muffled by Alec's presence. "It's a reference to one of Amalie's short stories, 'Black Velvet Vixen.' I'm not sure how it's supposed to relate to me." She gave him a questioning look, her eyes half-lidded. "I mean, a vixen is a shrew, a harridan...?"

Her cheeks grew warm when Alec smiled. He had a

lovely smile, slow and stealthy but really quite devastating to a female nervous system that had already snapped to attention and was now saluting like a Green Beret.

"Do you have a copy of the book?" he asked, so coaxingly she wondered if he'd ever been a snake charmer. He was petting her, too, she realized, his caress comforting as he dropped his previous no-nonsense manner for this sweet, soft persuasion.

Baffled, she said, "Over by the sofa," and while he retrieved the book, she used his short absence to gather her wits. There was something strange about the way he was treating her.

Then Alec was back, kneeling in front of her, both of his forearms pressed against her thighs as he rested his elbows on the chair, holding the book in her lap. She blinked, trying to tame the heady sense of arousal his nearness provoked. At least until she'd figured him out.

He opened *Black Velvet II* to the table of contents.

Lacey wet her lips. "You didn't learn this in the military," she said, sounding pretty tough except for the wobble in her voice.

Alec kept his head down. "Pardon?"

"It was smooth, I'll give you that. But overdone." She set her jaw with a click of her teeth. "I couldn't swallow it."

"I don't know what you—ah, here it is." He held up the book, opened to the correct page.

"Quite a skill. Taming the Hysterical and/or Recalcitrant Female. Did they teach it at spy school?"

Alec froze. She plucked the velveteen book out of his hand and dropped it to the carpet, confronting him with her frank stare. His eyes were not black, after all. Under the intense illumination from her makeup mirror, his pupils had shrunk to tiny dots and she could see that his irises were the dark, muddy brown of burnt tobacco. Faint lines radiated from the corners of the downturned eyelids, which gave his face a slightly melancholy cast. She put his age at mid- to late-thirties.

"Why did you say that?" he asked with no real expression, but much control in his taut voice.

She was confused again. "What? Oh. D'you mean the part about spy school? I was just kidding..." Her eyes widened. "Gosh. Don't tell me you really were a spy!"

"Of course not." He quickly glanced away, but she'd already seen his relief and found it rather odd. Out of context. "Where's that book?" he said, needlessly, as he was already picking it up. "You lost my place."

Quid pro quo, she thought, making note of his curious reaction before returning to her own place in the conversation. Alec Danieli was proving to be a very distracting bodyguard. "You can stop touching me now," she said stoutly, against all her instincts. "And no more soothing tones, please. I've calmed down." Though not entirely, it seemed.

A hint of admiration crossed Alec's face as he withdrew. "Usually they don't even realize," he murmured.

Lacey's brows arched. "They don't realize that you're taming them at the same time you're worming information out of them?"

He didn't answer.

"That's because you're terribly good at it. Not that your tricks worked on me, you understand." She crossed her arms over her chest. "I'm still not completely persuaded to your point of view. Which means I won't be wearing any disguises, but I will probably accept you as my bodyguard." She eyed him uncertainly. "For the time being."

He relaxed back against the sofa cushions. "You won't even know I'm here, Ms. Longwood."

"That'll be the day." Lacey laughed and spun her chair around to face the mirror, intending to check her makeup, but instead finding her gaze pulled relentlessly toward Alec's stark features and mesmerizing eyes. Although he held Amalie's book open on his lap, he was watching her watch him watch her.

Animal attraction sliced through Lacey's glossy composure like the swipe of a grizzly bear's paw, shredding all of her usual defenses. While she wasn't altogether convinced that she needed a bodyguard, it was suddenly acutely obvious that she *wanted* one.

3

Daniels kissed her!

At first Laryssa didn't like it. Such high-handed presumption was thoroughly insulting. But then the illicit thrill of the hard, cold kiss inundated her senses and she changed her mind. Her lashes fluttered shut. She opened her lips to find the supple, welcoming warmth of his mouth, murmuring her approval for him to continue.

And *then* he stopped!

He put his hands around her waist and set her back on her heels, so forcefully she nearly toppled over into the snowbank. "Keep away from me, little girl," he said—as if *she* had started it!

Laryssa stuttered with shock—and frustration. "D-D-Daniels...how dare you." She stamped her boot. "How dare you!"

LACEY HAD TO SPEAK to several production assistants before she got approval, but once it was understood that Alec was her bodyguard, he was sent to get a visitor's pass that would allow him on the set as long as he kept quiet and out of the way. He'd left his coat in the dressing room, so he clipped the pass to the pocket of his jeans and stood by to watch Lacey perform.

They were shooting the final scene of her initial run as Velvet Valancy. Lacey had explained that she would be back in several weeks once the extended contract was signed and Velvet's new story line established. In the meantime, she was doing a goodbye scene with the actor who played Case, whom Velvet had seduced in the hot tub and was now casting aside.

"I have to give you up," the Velvet character intoned, wrenching herself out of Case's manly arms. "You must return to your wife's bedside."

The actor playing Case took a few steps down the hospital-corridor set, then turned and looked back at her with regret. "I know what we did was wrong, but…" A sob caught in his throat. "I'll always remember you, Velvet Valancy."

Oh, man, Alec said silently.

One of the cameras zoomed in on Lacey, standing with her arms open, statuesque in a tight black velvet cat suit, glittery vest and silver boots. A perfect tear glistened in her eye. "And I'll always remember…" she took a deep breath, her breasts swelling admirably as she clasped her hands beneath her chin "…the hot tub."

"Cut," yelled the director, and suddenly the set was swarming with people. A makeup guy hurried over to blot Lacey's tear before it leaked into her mascara.

"Oh, cripes, will somebody puh-leeze give me a break."

Alec turned toward the woman standing beside him and gave her a questioning look. She was wearing a hospital gown and a droopy robe; several yards of gauze were wrapped around her head.

"What's with this crappy story line?" she asked rhetorically. "Here I am, just back from my honeymoon, and look at me—!" She gestured at her unbecoming getup. "*I* should be getting all the attention. Instead I'm in a freakin' coma!"

"Uh..." Alec said, trying to remember the name of the character the actress played.

"I'm just as good-gol'damn-looking as Madame X, aren't I?"

"Er..." Alec said. She had two fake but gruesome black eyes and was wearing pale, deathbed makeup.

The actress snapped a lightweight cast onto her left forearm and waved it in the air as she walked off. "*Someone's* gonna get leveled with this thing if I don't come out of that damn coma by the end of the week!"

And Lacey didn't think she needed a bodyguard? Alec laughed quietly to himself as the cameras rolled for another take. Hell hath no fury like an actress scorned. They were going to have to consider the possibility that Lacey's *All That Glitters* rival might be unhappy enough about being upstaged to make an attempt to prevent Velvet Valancy's return to the soap opera.

After another hour of stops and starts, the scene was finally finished. Lacey took a turn around the set, passing out hugs and kisses and goodbyes to the crew, then strutted back to her dressing room, with Alec trailing behind her. Watching her hips swing in time with the clickety-clack of her silver stiletto heels, he forgot he was her bodyguard. Hell, he forgot everything but how much he suddenly wanted to wrap his hands around her hips—her rear end was round and tight, the best he'd seen in a year—and pull her up hard against himself and show her how a clever man said goodbye. Or hello, for that matter.

Then he reminded himself—again—that he was only her bodyguard. That there was anything else on his mind probably just meant that he'd gone one year too long with only horses' hindquarters to look at.

He'd do well to remember that he was here to save

Madame X's butt...not commit debauched acts of lust upon it.

She was leaning over the dressing table to trowel cream onto her stage makeup, her wide eyes—impossibly blue in contrast with the white glop that masked her face—staring at him via the mirror. The heat that had been rising in Alec ever since he'd viewed the videotape was brought to a simmering boil. Why did she keep *looking* at him like that?

"I have to change," she said, using half a box of tissues to wipe off the face cream.

He backed up. "I'll step out, then."

"No. You can help me get this stuff packed. Why don't you, oh..." She spun in a circle, arms lifting as she reached back and pulled her hair into a ponytail. Her breasts shifted correspondingly beneath the black velvet that covered her bountiful curves as tightly as a pelt, and suddenly the sinuous sheen and undulant length of her had gotten Alec as hard as a brick.

"Here." She spied an overnight bag and tossed it at him. "Sweep all the junk off the dressing table into that. I've got to go through these heaps of black velvet—some of it's mine, some of it goes back to the costume department." Ripping off the glitzy vest, she stepped into the curtained closet and dressing area, then looked back at the silent, unmoving Alec. "You okay?"

"Yeah, sure."

She smiled and started peeling the cat suit off her shoulders. "I'm a bit of a pack rat."

He dragged his gaze away. "Well, I'm a bodyguard, not a lady's maid, so hurry it up."

She jerked the curtain closed. "Grou*cheee*."

Two seconds later her voice floated out from behind the curtain, pretend-tiny with abject humility. "I suppose this means you won't hand me the sweater I left out there?"

Alec hesitated, picturing her dashing out from behind the curtain half-undressed. Much as he'd have liked that, he made himself snatch up the first sweater at hand and thrust it through the gap between the curtain and the wall. Too much of a gap. Lacey's bare arm uncurled as she reached for the sweater, giving him enough of a glimpse to ascertain that she hadn't yet taken to wearing black velvet bras...only beige lace ones that dipped dangerously low—

"Thanks," she said, her voice jump-starting his brain. He backed away from the curtain as though it were a coiled cobra.

"Did you get everything?"

I got plenty, he thought. *More than I needed, but still not nearly enough to be satisfying.*

"Alec?"

"Yup," he said, sweeping his arm across the dressing table so her assorted beauty products tumbled into the open satchel. He plucked a dozen photographs from around the edges of the mirror and thumbed through them. For professional purposes.

Most of them were group shots. Lacey stood out among the various crowds of family, friends or fellow actors like a gilded lily in a vase of wildflowers. He tucked the photos into the bag's side pocket. Later, he'd ask her to identify the people in them; it was always possible that someone close to her held a grudge.

She came out from behind the curtain, doing up the gold buttons of the oversize black cardigan. Alec took one quick look and turned to snatch up the items remaining on the dressing table. While that big, floppy sweater of hers should have been decent, he was afraid it was going to slip off her shoulders at the slightest shrug. The tight burgundy skirt was not remotely acceptable; it was the size of a postage stamp. And her legs…

Alec couldn't bear to think about her legs.

"What, no black velvet?" he said gruffly.

She shrugged. The sweater slid along the slope of her pale bare shoulder, revealing a beige bra strap, the neckline widening until just in the nick of time she tugged it back into place. "Maybe I'm wearing black velvet undies."

Alec didn't respond. Keeping secrets was his stock-in-trade.

"Anyway," she said, fishing a pair of crumpled leather-and-velvet boots out from beneath the sofa, "will these do?" She sat to pull them on, leaving the black velvet shafts scrunched around her ankles like thick, wadded socks. He couldn't make himself look away, even after she caught him watching. She hugged her knees. Her toes tapped dancingly and the cardigan gaped and her lashes fluttered and, worst of all, her rose-colored lips curved into a flirtatious smile that made something cold and hard inside him go warm and soft. It was so disconcerting a sensation that he wondered if it was still possible to persuade Jericho to let him out of this job.

"What's this?" he asked abruptly, grasping at straws to distract himself from his own susceptibility.

Lacey got up and glanced at the framed photo he'd taken from the dressing table. "Me and my mom." Wrinkling her nose, she peered at her bare face in the mirror. "May I have my lipstick and mascara, please?"

Alec dumped the bag on the dressing table. "You look good enough without them."

"Eloquently put." Her gaze slipped several times toward him as she took out a lipstick and colored her lips a red so deep and dark her mouth glistened like chocolate-covered cherries. "But thank you."

Alec swallowing thickly. "The photograph...?"

"Little Miss Supercharm International, 1982. I won a trophy that was twice my height. My mother still polishes it every week."

"Oh." He finally looked at the photograph. It showed Lacey at ten, in full makeup and tiara and triumph, wearing a dress that could have housed a family of five under its pastel bouffant skirt. The ecstatic blond woman crouched beside Little Miss Supercharm International looked like beauty-contest material herself.

"Oh, you were one of those," he said.

"I know what you think."

His first thought was that now he better understood her stubborn reliance on her looks. Secondly, he thought it was astonishing that the impossible sapphire shade of her irises was natural. Unless she'd worn colored contacts even as a child...

"It wasn't like that," Lacey said. She released the ponytail and shook her head from side to side, then tousled her hair with artful fingers. "Not entirely."

Alec put the photograph inside the satchel and zipped it up. "Ready to go?"

"Just because I was a child beauty contestant, you're thinking I must be all screwed up in the head." She disappeared behind the curtain and came out with a garment bag and an overstuffed parachute duffel. "You think my values are superficial and the mirror my only source of self-esteem." She slung the strap of the duffel sideways across his chest, then piled the garment bag and satchel in his arms, adding a black velvet cape with tassels and a squashy black velvet hat with a peacock feather stuck in the crown. He wiggled his nose, snorting the feather aside. "You think that I trade on my beauty, that I crave attention and publicity, that I'm addicted to glamour." Satisfied that she'd turned Alec from the bodyguard she didn't want to the Sherpa she did, she eyed him challengingly. "Tell me, Danieli, is that what you think?"

"I..."

She tipped up her regal chin, her eyes flashing their magnificent blue fire. "Well, darlin', if you do," she said expansively, her arms thrown wide, "you're absolutely correct!"

Alec watched dumbfounded as she sashayed out the door.

LACEY LED THE WAY into the restaurant, too, even though Alec told her he should go first to scope out the lay of the land. She simply smiled sweetly at him and took off on her own when he turned to consult with the maître d'. Satisfied that her showy entrance had caused a stir among the patrons, she greeted Amalie and Jericho vociferously and slid into their horseshoe-shaped corner banquette.

Jericho and Alec nodded at each other and shook hands, apparently believing that a firm grip communicated more than words. *Men,* Lacey thought, and leaned back, waiting to see where Alec would choose to sit.

He sat opposite her.

"Neat-o, Alec," she said. "Boy, girl, boy, girl, just like my twelfth birthday party." She twined her arms around Jericho and leaned her chin on his shoulder. "Jericho, sweetie, you were a dear for thinking of me, but *where* did you find this man?"

Although he'd loosened up considerably since his marriage, Thomas Janes Jericho was not much of a tease; he took the question seriously. "At a besieged embassy in the Middle East, less than two years ago."

Lacey regarded Alec through narrowed eyes. "Hmm, yes, I can see that. There's a mysterious, sheik-ish air about him, isn't there? But you must explain fur-ther. I'm still not certain that I want to keep even a be-douin bodyguard. Maybe you can convince me."

Alec smiled thinly, which Lacey considered to be quite a feat with *his* lips. "Would you care to review my resumé, Ms. Longwood?"

She nodded. "For a start."

"Lacey—what—?" Amalie sputtered. "What are you up to now?" She turned to Alec, whom she'd met earlier that day when he and Jericho had consulted at their hotel. "She's putting you on, Alec. I'm afraid you'll have to learn to ignore her dramatics, as the rest of us have. And call her Lacey, why don't you?"

Lacey sniffed. "I rather enjoy being called Ms. Long-wood."

"Then we'll stick to that," said Alec. "I prefer it, my-self."

"Do you." Lacey unwound her arms from Jericho. "I'm so glad we're in agreement," she cooed, intending to needle him with her smooth-as-cream tone. Instead it clotted in her throat. So he wanted to keep his dis-tance from her, huh? Another mean feat, considering that he was her bodyguard.

Amalie and Jericho exchanged looks.

"I'd like a drink," Lacey said, keeping an eye on Alec even while she searched for a waiter. Alec was so cool and calm she wanted to goose him. She wanted sparks to fly. "Why aren't we dining at Lutece or the Four Sea-sons—someplace with a little class?"

"Cut the prima donna act," Alec snapped, and Lacey

whipped her head around. He was not smiling. "Being 'seen' is no longer your top priority."

Earnestly Amalie agreed. "He's right, you know." She looked a little green around the gills at the chance that someone could be spying on them even as they spoke.

Lacey was not so timid. "Have these fussbudgets convinced you, too, Am? Shoot, think of all the fan letters you've received since the first *Black Velvet* book was published. Scads of them were on the weird side, to put it politely, and *you* haven't been harmed."

Amalie conceded the point. "I don't take any chances, though."

"Walking into a nice, expensive restaurant isn't risky to anything but my pocketbook." Lacey cast a sidelong look at Alec and slipped into her heaviest Southern accent. "'Specially now that Jericho has hired me a li'l ole bodyguard of my very own."

"Then you're willing to cooperate with Alec?" Jericho said, smothering another grin.

Lacey was glad that *someone* knew she was doing her Madame X act on purpose. She leaned over the table to send Alec a puckered-lips air kiss. "I expect that depends on what all he asks me to do...."

"Heavens, Lacey—behave yourself." Amalie shook her head at such outrageousness. "Alec's a good guy. Stop yanking his chain."

"Oh, all right, but I do want that drink." Lacey looked again for a waiter. "Danieli, my good man," she said, "here's your chance to be of service."

Alec's mouth quirked, but he put up his hand and almost at once two waiters converged on the table wielding tiny parchment menus. Alec extended his palm to indicate Lacey's need for assistance, and the waiters must have recognized her because suddenly they were falling all over themselves to meet her every desire.

Comforted that there were still some benefits to fame, Lacey ordered a bottle of chardonnay and shooed the waiters away. Her lashes flicked at sober Alec. "I suppose you don't drink on the job?"

His answer was a deadpan "Only if I really need to."

She was always willing to laugh at herself. "Then working for Madame X should qualify." Alec must have agreed; he accepted a full glass when the wine arrived.

Forcing herself to think of appetizers instead of appetite, Lacey held her menu near the dinky candlestick lamp at the center of the table and squinted at the spidery calligraphy describing the specials.

Alec was *still* watching her. "Vision problems, Ms. Longwood?" he asked. "I thought you wear contacts?"

"My eyesight is perfect. It's just so dark in here."

"Then your eyes are real."

She blinked. "And also my hair," she said. "Mostly."

His gaze skipped lower for the briefest of looks, but she caught his meaning just the same. "They're real, too," she said dryly, and defiantly squared her shoulders. Heck, she'd survived a hundred persnickety judges on cellulite patrol, so she should be able to handle the insinuations of one darkly saturnine male.

Amalie and Jericho exchanged another look, then moved a little closer to each other and began to study their menus with an intensely silent concentration. Although Lacey suspected that their bowed heads hid grins of amusement, she didn't mind. She was having fun, too. Who'd have guessed that a bodyguard could be so…entertaining?

Her eyes traced the hawkish lines of Alec's candlelit

profile as he turned to speak to one of the hovering waiters. *And provocative*, she silently added with a delicate shiver. She hadn't expected that, either.

By the time appetizers had been distributed around the table, Jericho and Alec were discussing Lacey's problem in earnest. "I'm taking Amalie back to the island tomorrow," Jericho said. "She'll be safe there."

Smiling gently, Amalie brushed her new husband's long, sand-colored hair back from his collar and fed him a bite of sourdough bread. "We both will."

He turned his head and bitingly kissed her palm. "Right."

"Okay, break it up, people." Laughing, Lacey paused midway through her attack on her bluepoint oysters. "The honeymoon's over."

"Not for another ten months," Amalie said. "Jericho promised me that if I'd agree to a quick wedding without any fuss, he'd see to it that the honeymoon lasted for a whole year."

"Then it's a good thing you're heading back to Belle Isle." Having consumed most of her oysters, Lacey eyed Alec's appetizer as she reached for her wineglass. "Too much exposure to this lovey-dovey stuff always makes me want to go out and get naked with…" there was an almost imperceptible hesitation as her glance passed from Alec's food to Alec "…a he-man like Lars Torberg. He was a real, swinging, Me-Tarzan-You-Jane kinda guy."

"Lars Torberg?" Alec said, grudgingly curious.

"The B-movie action star."

Alec's expression betrayed no envy, but Lacey knew he had to be seething inside. What man wouldn't? Lars was tall, blond and built. It was also true that his brain was as thick and quick as an iceberg, but some things a bodyguard didn't have to know.

"Did you part on good terms?"

The glitter in Lacey's eyes dimmed. If Alec was thinking only of business, there was no sport in making him jealous. "A mutual breakup," she admitted. "No motive there."

"I don't know...." Amalie contemplated. "I've stepped on the trail of your broken hearts before, Lacey. Lars might have cared more than you think."

Lacey chuckled. "Maybe he'd be capable of sending a mash note, but a semifamous, six-five Nordic hunk skulking around a bookstore, defacing copies of *Black Velvet II*? I don't see it."

"Neither do I," Alec said. But there was a peculiar look on his face as he watched her steal a bite of his baked Brie. "Do you have any enemies?"

"Only every understudy in every play I ever starred in." She reached over with a knife and a cracker and he pushed the plate toward her. "And every runner-up in every beauty pageant I ever won."

"How about someone with connections to *Black Velvet* and Madame X?"

"There are the folks we know at Pebblepond Press." Lacey glanced at Amalie. "Norris Yount and Minette Styles, the publicist. But they're not enemies, of course."

"Rosie Bass, my editor," Amalie said.

"And Harry Bass," Jericho contributed, to be fair. Harry was his editor at *NewsProfile* magazine; they'd broken the story about the truth behind the Madame X pseudonym.

"Harry and Rosie—are they related?" Alec asked.

"They're divorced...."

"Adversaries?" Alec queried, mulling over a possible motive of revenge.

"We think they're getting back together," Amalie

said, crossing her fingers. "They seemed pretty tight when they came to Belle Isle for the wedding."

Alec sighed. "We need to pinpoint someone with reason to hate one of you."

"I thought we'd agreed that the threats were directed at me," Lacey said, alarmed for her friend if not herself. Amalie was a meek, gentle soul. She couldn't defend herself the way Lacey could.

Again Jericho put his arm around dainty Amalie; the reaction seemed to be a reflex. "Yes, but 'Madame X' could actually refer to either of you, so we have to consider every possibility to be safe."

Alec snapped his fingers impatiently. "Enemies, enemies," he said, prompting Lacey.

"I stepped on a few toes at Pebblepond Press during the course of the *Black Velvet* book tour. For instance, Minette, the publicist, wasn't pleased with a couple of interviews I did after the truth broke about our charade. And they didn't take to my agent's threat that they'd lose me as Madame X if they didn't start paying me what I was worth." Lacey stared at the plate of cheese, walnuts and sautéed apples, no longer hungry. "There's my former agent, Bennett Cooper—I dumped him for Piper Hicks. And Laszlo, an old roommate who still owes me back rent. He recently looked me up, thinking I could get him a part on *All That Glitters*—"

"And the book critic from the *New York Express!*" Amalie interjected, suddenly remembering. "When the truth about Madame X came out, he was very angry. He said we'd made a fool of him."

"This sounds promising." Alec was scribbling the names they'd mentioned in a small notebook. "Tell me more."

Lacey shrugged. "That critic was a simp. A pompous windbag in a bow tie. Nothing to fear there. I could snap him like a twig."

Amalie giggled. "What about Bob Slob, the deejay in Chicago? You ground *him* beneath your spike heel."

"Kevin Kincaid, the talk show host," added Jericho. "She turned him down for a date, on the air. His ego was decimated."

Alec tossed up his hands. "So what you're saying is the entire populace has reason to dislike, envy or revile Madame X."

"Sheesh," Lacey blurted, trying to make a joke of it. "And here I thought Madame X was only admired, ogled and beloved."

Alec was being entirely serious. "There's a thin line between love and hate, especially with an obsessive personality."

"Okay, okay. Y'all are starting to get me scared." Lacey glowered at Alec, her fists clenched atop the table. "Is that what you wanted?"

"If it makes you more reasonable, yes." His stare was measuring. "Perhaps now would be a good time to discuss when you'll leave the city."

"What?" Lacey rapped the tabletop in disbelief. "Wait a minute, buster. First you want me to get ugly and now you want me to run away?" She started to wave her arms but had to stop to grab a handful of the loose neckline of her chenille sweater. "Well, listen up—and try to understand this time. I have a contract. Two of them. I have fans. Commitments. A career!"

"You have a potential stalker. All I'm trying to do is prevent—"

"Forget it," Lacey snapped, her cheeks flushed as she slid out of the banquette and rose majestically to her feet. The most important lesson she'd learned from her years of pageants and auditions was that you didn't give up your dream so easily. "Let me tell you this, Danieli—I may only think I don't need a body-guard, but I definitely *know* I don't need a dictator!"

Alec couldn't help but whistle in wordless admiration as he watched her stalk off in the direction of the ladies' room with her chin leading the way, her long stride eating up the carpet and her loose hair floating across her shoulders like a golden banner.

Amalie murmured "Excuse me," and scurried to catch up to her friend. Jericho looked at Alec.

Alec looked at Jericho, his mouth twitching into a grin. "That Madame X is a real pistol, isn't she?" One hand scrubbed the lower half of his face as if to wipe away the grin. "I think I'm going to hate you for getting me into this."

Jericho decided it was too soon to gloat. But he did say, "Someday, Alec, you're going to thank me."

LACEY BANGED THROUGH the door of the peach-and-ivory-striped ladies' room, her head held high. "That man infuriates me!"

Amalie caught the swinging door. "Probably because you haven't yet been able to wind him around your little finger."

Lacey glared at the mirror over the washbasins, stabbing her fingers into her hair and fluffing it by the roots. She stuck up her pinkies like tiny horns. "I can wind *any* man, darlin'. This one might need to be taught some flexibility first, but then he'll corkscrew just as pretty as you please." She poked her tongue out at her reflection, then spun away from the mirror.

Amalie shook her head. "Oh, Lacey, you're being so mean to him, and he only has your best interests at heart. I don't see why you can't cooperate. Make nice, not war, okay? Let him see the real you, not just the drama-queen you."

Lacey cocked her head, looking at Amalie with softened eyes. "Alec's only the hired gun. It's you and Jericho who want what's best for me. And I appreciate it. But, Am…" She shuddered. "I don't want to need a bodyguard!"

Amalie nodded. Lacey hadn't said she didn't *need* a bodyguard, nor that she didn't *want* one. Only that she didn't want to need one. And that told Amalie a lot about her usually upbeat friend's state of mind.

There was a padded bench placed against one wall, and Lacey suddenly went to sit on it, hunching her shoulders forward and burying her face in her hands. "I really hate this," she moaned. "I won't stand for it."

Amalie sat, too, making soothing noises while she patted Lacey's shoulder. "Go ahead, let out all your frustrations. I know the pressure of the situation must be making you crazy."

After a minute, Lacey put her elbows on her knees and sighed heavily. "I suppose I could ease up on Alec. None of this mess is his fault."

"That's right." Amalie tugged at the collar of the gaping sweater. "And you know what else?" she clucked. "You should have worn a blouse or camisole under this sweater. Or were you testing your new bodyguard to see how easily he could be distracted?"

A short laugh burst from Lacey like a hiccup. "How well you know me."

"I know that beneath that brash glamour-girl exterior is a heart as big and good and sweet as a stack of pancakes soaked in maple syrup." With a motherly gesture Amalie brushed Lacey's hair back from her face. "I just wish you'd let Alec Danieli know it, too."

Lacey shrugged. Her expression was still abnormally bleak.

"And I also know that you must be very worried. And scared, too."

Lacey's eyes widened. "What makes you say that?"

"We both know that Alec only means to help. You wouldn't be giving him quite such a hard time if the situation wasn't eating at you inside. You're always most flamboyant when you're trying to avoid a harsh reality." Amalie nudged her friend. "Like the time you held a huge Halloween party at your apartment the very night before you were going to be evicted for overdue rent. You put together a costume of Monopoly money, only the glue didn't hold...."

"And the guests started matching every paper dollar I shed with a bill of the real thing." Lacey produced a dry chuckle. "I not only made the rent, I got a job offer from a strip club owner."

"Why, Lacey, I'm shocked. You never told me that part of the story."

"Don't worry, Am. I got a big modeling job in St. Bart's the very next day and then I was flush for another few months. I never had to resort to stripping. Not that it wouldn't have been an interesting experience, mind you."

Although Amalie *tsk-tsked* scoldingly, the light of *Black Velvet* inspiration twinkled in her eyes. Lacey's adventures—and misadventures—were a constant source of ideas.

Lacey sighed again. "Anyway..."

Amalie nodded. "None of that changes our present predicament."

"I really don't think you're the target, Amalie."

"Probably not, but you know Jericho. He's sticking

to me like a prickly burr all the same. We'll both feel better once we're back on the island."

"Nobody could get to you there. But even the remote possibility kind of kills the mood of your extended honeymoon, doesn't it?"

"Well, now..." Amalie's cheeks turned a mottled pink. "There is the fact that Jericho's sticking to me like a prickly burr," she said in her delicate way.

They both laughed, then quickly sobered. The hatefully detailed threats of the anonymous letters had made their usually frequent laughter seem forced. After an awkward moment of silence, Amalie excused herself to enter one of the stalls.

Okay, so maybe Am's right, Lacey admitted to herself. She was taunting Alec because she'd do almost anything not to have to face up to the potentially violent reality of the letter-writer's intent. Running off her bodyguard was just another version of her favorite defense mechanism. Out of sight equaled out of mind. And out of mind equaled out of danger, which was a stubbornly blind sort of syllogism, but, hey, whatever worked....

And what if that meant she'd be left alone to dance on her own grave? How entertaining would she find that?

On the other hand, she was already certain that keeping Alec Danieli around would be hazardous to her state of mind in a whole other way. Not to mention the state of her body.

Still, better Alec-take-me-to-bed than...*dead*.

Lacey stood and tried to work up a smile for the glamour girl reflected back at her. She swiped the tip of a finger over her smudged mascara, recalling that her loopy country grandma used to say that dealing with the devil in your hand was better than the two in the bush.

And she'd always found a certain cockeyed wisdom in Grandma Lacey-Beth's advice.

ALEC PICKED AT A SLICE of apple smeared with Brie, wondering if he should go and check out the ladies' room. A serious bodyguard would. But clearly Lacey Longwood wasn't serious about having her body guarded. She'd probably screech at him to mind his own business and then slam his head in the swinging door for good measure.

"At least you're still smiling," Jericho said, and Alec stopped because up to then he hadn't realized that he was. "Seven hours with Lacey is enough to send plenty of guys packing."

Alec cocked an eyebrow.

"She's like a hot fudge sundae," Jericho continued. "Very tempting. Very rich and sweet and—"

"Nutty."

Jericho chuckled. "My point was that she can be too much. Men are eager to indulge at first, but eventually they blanch at the idea of a steady diet of hot fudge sundaes."

Alec didn't know what prompted him to say, "I might be developing a sweet tooth." Probably the same wayward impulse that made him smile at the thought of her slamming his head in the rest room door.

"Well," Jericho said, rubbing his chin. "That's rather surprising."

I wasn't really serious. "I'm serious," Alec said.

They sat in silence for a long while. Finally Jericho cleared his throat. "And here I was worried that, uh…that you might…"

"Decline the assignment?" Alec glanced toward the rest rooms for the fiftieth time. "I probably should."

Jericho waited.

"But I do owe you one."

Jericho waited some more.

"If it hadn't been for your series of articles on the embassy scandal in Zhabekistan, I might be spending the next millenium in the lockup."

"Nah," Jericho said. "The military investigators would have cleared you once they'd caught and skinned the Cat." At Alec's grim expression, he gave a wry grin. "That was a pun. A joke. Supposed to be funny."

Alec didn't even blink. "Does Lacey remind you of Cat Szako?"

Jericho looked stunned. "Not in the least."

"It must be all in my mind, then."

"Superficially, I suppose, there's a resemblance...."

Alec's thoughts turned inward. Nineteen months ago he'd discovered that the woman he'd been dating, a pretty blond European freelancing as an interpreter in the Mideast, had in fact been a Russian-Romanian expatriate spy hired by the Iranians to acquire privileged information on the U.S. defense of Zhabekistan's crucial twenty miles of Caspian Sea coastline. Whereas Cat's wiles hadn't succeeded with Alec, the ensuing investigation had revealed that they'd apparently worked on two of the marine security guards. Which had put Alec, in Zhabekistan on a top secret clearance, but ostensibly there as the embassy's superior officer, under an equal suspicion of treason.

Rightfully, he admitted to himself, even now feeling culpable for his breached authority. Still, his military career might have survived in some form if only more members of the media than Jericho had understood the vast difference between "under investigation" and "guilty as charged." After Alec had been torn to bits by the press corps, and investigators had officially "cleared" what was left, his only consolation had been an honorable discharge. And his only escape from notoriety a small horse farm tucked far away in the foothills of the Blue Ridge Mountains.

"But the resemblance is only slight," Jericho continued. "Trust me."

Alec nodded. Jericho was one of the very few people that he did trust.

Whereas Madame X was…Madame X. And she was coming this way. "If I survive this woman," Alec said out of the corner of his mouth to Jericho, "never ask me for another favor as long as I live."

4

Daniels didn't respond. He merely turned his back on her and lifted a stack of gift boxes out of the trunk.

Part of Laryssa wanted to demand his apology. But another part of her felt his kiss rolling through her like a rare bolt of winter thunder. She tilted her face to the snow falling from the leaden sky and took a deep breath. Snowflakes melted on her parted lips.

"Daniels," she said, her voice thick and soft with the knowledge of how much she wanted him. How much she'd always wanted him.

"Yes, Miss Laryssa?" Finally she knew he wasn't as detached as he sounded.

"I am twenty-two years old, Daniels."

He eyed her over the top of the boxes without speaking. Still, she could read the heat of his male response as she approached, her boots crunching on the snow.

"I am a woman," she said, and the gift boxes tumbled from his arms as she took his hand, stripped off the glove and boldly slid his fingers up under her long taffeta skirt.

"WHAT WAS THAT ABOUT hot fudge sundaes?" Lacey asked as she let herself and Alec into her new apartment in a pre–World War II brick building of faded, funky glory. On a surge of fiscal optimism, she'd signed a lease on the same day that Piper Hicks, Inc. had taken her on as a client. Due to Manhattan prices, this apartment was her first solo.

"I don't know what you mean."

"Why did Jericho want us to order hot fudge sundaes for dessert? He doesn't even like hot fudge sundaes."

Alec's eyes were scanning the high-ceilinged, three-room apartment like the X-ray machine at the airport.

"I like hot fudge sundaes," he murmured. He took in the yellowed wallpaper and scarred woodwork without comment, then stuck his head inside her bedroom door.

Lacey hadn't figured he was the hot fudge sundae type. "Is that a joke? Because I've probably got a jar of Smucker's in the fridge if you—"

"Stay there," he barked, as preemptory as the worst drill sergeant. He disappeared into the dark bedroom.

Naturally, she rushed over to see what was up.

Looking sheepish, he emerged with the velvet hat she'd dropped off earlier along with the rest of her things from the dressing room. "False alarm."

"Well, you're cautious, I'll give you that. First a deadly black velvet thong, now a lethal peacock feather…" She chuckled. "Gosh, Alec, what would I do without you to save me from my clothing?" *Now if only he'd consent to peel her out of her tight miniskirt before it cut off her circulation.*

"It was perched on top of that thing—that body thing. How was I to know—"

She grabbed the hat. "That's Countess Pushkin. She's a dressmaker's dummy, a leftover from one of my roommates who was a fashion design student until she fell in with a bad crowd of English lit majors."

Alec turned on his heel and eyed the row of papier-mâché trees she'd set up behind the moth-eaten love seat that, other than a new queen-size bed, was her only semicomfortable piece of furniture. "Unusual decor," he said, and sat on one of her many large unpacked cardboard boxes as if the sight of jawbreakers and peppermint swirls glued to fake trees had taken his knees out.

Lacey flopped onto the love seat, her body curved like an S. "This group I'm in, Nine Actors in Search of a Theatre, did an avant garde production of *Hansel and Gretel* in somebody's loft. I was the stepmother with issues."

Alec looked askance at a pair of eight-foot candy canes that flanked the kitchen doorway like columns. "And you took home the props."

"Electra-Gretel got the costumes."

"It must be like living in a life-size Candyland game."

"Wait'll you see the gingerbread bathroom," she said drolly. "Most of the furniture in my last apartment belonged to my roommate, but now that I'm earning good money, I can finally decorate on my own. What do you think of beaded lamps and a sleek red Italian couch? Velvet swags at the windows..."

He nodded. "Yes, that's more what I'd expect from the likes of Madame X."

"I knew you'd say that." She sucked in a breath and leaned forward, carelessly knocking a stack of mail across the love seat's sagging cushions. "But tell me. Are you making any distinction between us?"

He pulled back, startled. "Between you and me?"

While it was interesting that his mind had leaped to such a conclusion, she shook her head. "Me and Madame X. You do know that we're two separate entities?

She's a character. I am a woman." Alec had introduced the subject, so it was his fault that she was thinking up a million ways for him to make her even more of a woman. "I'm—" she gulped for more air, her throat as tight as her skirt "—a real woman, a flesh-and-blood woman."

He lowered his head and raked both hands through his hair, revealing a high forehead and a certain amount of trepidation. "You can say that again," he muttered, carefully not looking at her.

"I already did, darlin'." Lacey slithered to her feet, suddenly concerned about their overnight arrangements. Was Alec supposed to be a twenty-four-hour bodyguard? It was one thing to flirt with him, another to share pajamas and pillows and toothpaste. Even though he'd fit exceedingly well into the bottoms of her plaid flannel jammies...

Unsure of where they stood with each other, Lacey glanced down to gauge Alec's expression. She blinked. Either she was imagining things or he was staring at her legs like a lonely soldier with a Betty Grable pinup. The chance that he might desire her as much as she desired him was thrilling...but perplexing. "Umm, Alec," she purred.

His fingers tightened in his hair, sweeping down to his nape before they released. "Yes, Ms. Longwood?"

She was brought up short by the name. "Okay, enough with that," she said, sidling away. "Call me Lacey."

He straightened, dark eyes glinting as they traced her retreat toward the bedroom. "Where are you going?"

"To slip into something more comfortable, as they say." She gave a token toss of her hair before slamming the door. A confused mix of emotional and physical needs was pinwheeling inside her, but there was nothing she could—or *should*—do about any of her impulses. Nothing safe, at any rate.

"Well, shoot," she whispered, stricken by the rare fact of Alec's unavailability. She almost always got what she wanted, but this time she was hesitating to ask, especially as Alec didn't seem all that cooperative. Which meant that here they were, awkwardly stuck together under terrifying circumstances, with two bodies meant for each other except for the problem of their stubborn wills, which would never mesh, not to mention her big mouth and his steely intentions, and boy oh boy what *was* she going to do with Alec for the night?

Grandma Lacey-Beth had been wrong. If the devil was in your hand he was already way too close.

Okay. Take it easy. Deep breaths, in and out. So they had a mutual attraction thing going. That was okay, more than okay, even if they couldn't act on it. Deeper breaths. *After all, it wasn't like he'd be a permanent fixture in her life. He only wanted to take charge until…*

Lacey clenched her hands. That was it; that's what was causing her consternation. She didn't want to be taken charge of, not even by a man who was sexy enough to make her think surrendering her body to him wouldn't be so bad. Would, in fact, be rather wonderful, and delicious, and shiveringly erotic.

The situation was similar to how she'd felt about hitting the beauty pageant circuit with her mom: just because she enjoyed herself while doing it didn't mean she wanted to give up everything else in order to continue.

Countess Pushkin loomed from the shadows in the corner. Not her best look under the circumstances. Lacey hit the lights and tossed the hat she'd been squashing in her fists toward the stump that topped the dummy's hourglass-shaped body. The countess would have to be relegated to the closet for the duration, but Lacey's first order of business was to squirm out of her spandex miniskirt. Surely then she'd be able to breathe normally. Even with Alec Danieli in the vicinity.

One door away. All night long. Sharing pajamas, pillows, toothpaste, kisses…

Well, maybe this one time familiarity would breed contempt. Though Grandma Lacey-Beth had always said, with a cackle and a wink, "Sweetie pie, familiarity just breeds."

ALEC WAS STILL FLOATING through a fantasy version of Candyland with a million miles of gorgeous leg wrapped around his imagination. *He could feel them, Lacey's legs, supple and strong, tightening around his waist as he sank into the melting velvet heart of her….*

"Oh, man," he whispered when he realized what he was doing. Hadn't Jericho warned him this might happen? Something about the corrupting influence of black velvet…? Alec had thought it was a joke.

Finally he forced himself to move, the cardboard box creaking beneath him as he shifted his weight. Out of habit, he began to straighten the disarray of Lacey's mail, most stuck with the yellow labels of her forwarding address. Out of suspicion, he rifled through the handful of envelopes.

One of them struck him as familiar, though it looked blameless enough. He held it by one corner, studying the precise block printing. Lacey's full name and new address. *Damn.*

Alec moved fast. "Lacey!" He rapped once and opened the door without waiting for her answer. A mistake. She was bent over at the waist, swiveling her hips, skinning the miniskirt down past her rump so that two smooth rounds of flesh rose like ivory moons from the restricting band of spandex.

He stopped, stunned, with only one thought registering in his brain: *Madame X's black velvet had nothing on Lacey's beige lace.*

"Hey!" she said.

"Sorry," he blurted, and slammed the door. He backed away, staring blankly, the sight of her half-naked and wiggling stamped forever in his memory like a fresh tattoo on a drunken marine. Indelible.

Before he could even begin to cool his shocking arousal, Lacey sauntered out of the bedroom, casually knotting the drawstring on a pair of loose, silky black pants. She gave him a bland smile. "We're going to have to set some ground rules if you expect to remain my bodyguard." She went into the kitchen, opened the fridge and called in a friendly, noncommittal voice, "Want some juice? It's papaya mango."

"No, thanks," he croaked. He should have been glad that at least one of them was playing the awkward situation in the right way—casual, unembarrassed, with a shrug that said *so what?*

Why, then, did it rankle that she was less affected than he?

Alec reminded himself that she was an actress and model. She was accustomed to stripping in front of virtual strangers, using her body as a tool, her face as a Get Out of Jail Free card. She could present any exterior she pleased to her chosen audience.

Just like Cat.

Lacey padded out of the kitchen. She lowered the glass of juice and licked her lips, watching him warily. "Something wrong? Cat got your tongue?"

Precisely, Alec said silently, and fast-froze his dark,

simmering desires. "I found this in your mail." He held out the envelope.

Lacey knew at once what it was. "I don't want it."

"I'll open it, then. It's already been handled, but we can still have it checked for prints tomorrow."

"Should I call the police?" She watched him use a sharply efficient pocketknife to slice open the envelope. "No, what's the use? They'll just say the same thing—they can't do anything until either the law or my head is actually broken." She laughed without humor. "Whichever comes first."

While Alec perused the letter, she went to curl up on the ratty love seat, her arms wrapped around her legs. She'd read enough of the previous letters to know how this one would go. What opened as an innocuous fan letter would soon degenerate into a diatribe of name-calling and physical threats, expressing the writer's "disappointment" that Madame X hadn't yet responded to his overtures.

Lacey shuddered. The worst parts were when the creep described in bloodcurdling detail what he'd do to her if she didn't stop flaunting herself in front of other men. He wanted her to pledge her loyalty to him alone.

Alec whistled softly through his teeth. "This guy's a nasty piece of work." He slid the letter back into the envelope, touching only the edges. "Are you certain that you haven't noticed anyone in particular at the *Black Velvet* events? According to some of these details, he's been there, watching you—"

"Don't," Lacey snapped. "You're just trying to scare me so I'll do everything you ask like a good little girl."

"Damn it, Lacey, I'm *protecting* you—"

"Yes, I know, but…" Her chin came up. "You'll have to do it without putting me in a cage."

Alec's eyes narrowed. "Woman, you're stubborn as a mule."

"Nope. Stubborn as a mugwump." She smiled a little at his questioning look and murmured, "Something my country grandma used to say."

He walked soundlessly to the closet. Lacey watched him put the letter into the pocket of his trench coat. He came to sit beside her, and she studied the seamless grace of his movements and the sliver of space between them with her heart banging in her chest.

"As opposed to your city grandma?" he asked softly.

"That's right. Grandma Stuart lived in Charleston, in a fancy antebellum house in the heart of the city. When my mother and I visited, we went to museums, concerts and ladies' teas in between lengthy shopping excursions." Lacey pressed her hands between her knees. "Grandma Lacey-Beth lived on a farm in the country. She shoveled out stalls, chopped heads off chickens and picked up squealing piglets by their tails. Fascinatingly awful to an eight-year-old, but I wasn't prepared to sacrifice my ruffled dresses and lace-edged anklets to participate."

"No one suggested overalls and rubber boots?"

"My mother didn't approve of dirt, and by the time I realized I might be of another opinion, it was too late. Except for the occasional foray into farm life, I was hooked on glamour and style."

Alec sat quietly, his hands on his thighs, fingers spread. Strong, working hands, Lacey thought, squeezing her knees tighter. Hands that were also careful and quick and as beautifully drawn as a Da Vinci. More so, really, because it was so easy to imagine them coming to life and skimming across her skin. She made a small sound in her throat and rested her chin on her knees, more aware than she needed to be of the rapid ticking of her pulse.

"So you're a city girl," he said. "I should have expected that."

Her bare toes wormed down between the cushions. "I like to maintain a certain level of comfort and convenience that usually clashes with rustic living."

He studied her, much as she had studied him. "Hmm."

The apartment was so silent that the blare of traffic from the street six stories down was audible. Suddenly Lacey lifted her head from her knees, mouth gaping. "You did it again!" she charged.

"What?" Alec asked, the innocence of his expression ruined by the smug tuck of his top lip.

"You purposely distracted me by making me talk about my grandmothers." It was frustrating to be so easily manipulated into distraction, but amusing, too, because he didn't know that he could accomplish the same thing by just sitting there and letting her stare at him. She smiled. "I suppose y'all were afraid one silly little letter was gonna give me hysterics."

"Well, you're calmer now, aren't you?"

She thought of her speeding pulse. "Relatively so."

He cleared his throat. "In that case, I need to ask you a few questions." When she nodded, he proceeded carefully. "I'm not trying to frighten you, but it's significant that this last letter was sent to your home address. Weren't the others part of the Madame X fan mail forwarded by Amalie's publishers?"

"Yes. There were three of them altogether. The first two were pretty mild, slightly creepy, but not scary. Then the third one was, well—"

"The 'vixen' letter. I read it."

Lacey averted her face. "There were two others I

didn't show to Jericho and Amalie. They were sent to me in care of *All That Glitters*. I, uh, threw them away."

She'd expected him to berate her for destroying evidence, but he only winced and said, "They were bad?"

She shrugged. "Pretty bad."

He nodded, as if that was no worse than he'd expected. "Then came the vandalism at the book signing, upping the stakes. And now Mr. X makes it clear to us that he knows your home address. You really need to be on your guard, Lacey. There's no telling what—"

"Well, that's your job, isn't it?" She tried to seem confident of—and comfortable with—his protection. "You're supposed to be prepared for anything, like a Boy Scout."

"Right. But I still need your cooperation."

She groaned. "Back to the wigs, glasses and padding?"

"Don't go off on me," he warned, holding up his hands.

Lacey smiled wanly. "Truth to tell, I'm beginning to see the wisdom in *not* looking like Madame X." She lightly punched at his palms, one-two, like a boxer. "Darn it, anyway."

"This is good," he started to say with relish, but she sprang to her feet.

"Don't get all Mussolini, now, Alec," she warned, while she brought her juice glass back to the kitchen. She turned on the radio—music would fill in their silences—and came out doing the cha-cha in her bare feet to a golden oldie from the Miami Sound Machine.

"I guess I didn't have to worry about you flipping out over the letter," Alec said, watching as she shimmied to the Latin beat.

She plopped down beside him with a flick of her honey-colored mane. "I don't see any use in fretting."

"Just as long as you're taking this seriously."

"Oh, Alec." She slid lower on her spine, stretching her legs out straight and wiggling her toes. She had the fidgets, and she had them bad. "It'd be difficult not to when there's a big lump of a bodyguard sitting on my sofa." She peered over at him, grinning at the look on his face, certain that no one had ever called the immaculate Alec Danieli "a big lump," not with his crisp trench coat and polished boots and tight, fit body. She remembered how precisely he'd wielded his knife and fork in the continental manner over his plate of healthy broiled fish, and how she'd sopped up marinara sauce with the last chunk of her garlic bread, probably dripping it down her cleavage without even noticing. Knowing that Alec would have—he seemed to notice everything—she tugged at her sweater and looked inside.

He made a choking noise. She looked up from her clean breasts and said blithely, "Just checking if they're still there."

"Do you have to do that often?" he asked, sounding as if the Boston Strangler had ahold of his throat.

She smoothed the sweater into place with a proprietary pat. "Two of Madame X's biggest assets, wouldn't you say?"

Alec shifted. "I detect a note of sarcasm."

She snorted. "Hey, you're the guy who wants to pad me out like a clown." Flirtatiously, she slung one of her legs across his and slid her toes up the black denim encasing his shin. "Maybe I can wear a pair of those huge, floppy clown shoes, too."

"It's late, and this is getting us nowhere," Alec said stiffly. He lifted her leg off his, holding it by the ankle with two fingers as if it was a stinky diaper he was heaving into the trash can. For a moment he hesitated, then pushed her leg off to the side and quickly retracted his hand.

Lacey sat up, legs crossed beneath her, two spots burning on her ankle as though it had been caught in a vise. So he wasn't interested. What a big, whopping lie!

Still, she shouldn't have been teasing him, not when fifteen minutes ago the thought of getting too close to him had set her emotions on purée. He was just so straight, so correct, so eminently teasable that she couldn't help herself.

"I can't sleep yet," she said. "I'm too keyed up. Why don't you tell me a little about yourself, since you still haven't given me that resumé."

"I don't do bedtime stories."

"Aw, c'mon." She curled into the cushions, her body wound into as small a package as she could make it, which admittedly wasn't all that small because her shins were still pressed against Alec's side. She nudged his thigh with her toes, and it was as firm as the look in his eyes.

"Quit it," he said.

She put one hand on his forearm, gave a squeeze and then danced her fingertips up to the sharp angle of his elbow. "I'll stop only if you keep me otherwise entertained."

"Divas," he said with a sneer, but she'd seen the light of interest that had momentarily flickered in his eyes.

"Have you been a bodyguard before?" she coaxed, to start him off.

He brushed away her hand. "In a manner of speaking."

She rolled her eyes. "What's that supposed to mean?"

"It means, no, I don't usually baby-sit starlets in my spare time."

"Then why are you here?"

"I told you. Jericho asked me for a favor."

She weighed that. "Judging by your attitude, you must have owed him a big one. A *really* big one."

"That's right."

"A humongous one."

"I'm not going to tell you what it was."

"Okay, then I'll guess. Something concerning…women?" The way that Alec's jaw jutted—she wondered if he'd brought a razor for his five o'clock shadow—made her dismiss the possibility of the favor involving women troubles. She couldn't picture either Alec or Jericho needing each other's help in that area. "It must be professional, then. But weren't you in the military—the marines? Jericho certainly wasn't. In fact, he's the kind of long-haired, independent-minded journalist who drives gung ho soldiers up the wall. So…?"

Alec sat stonily silent.

"Gee, you're no fun," she said with a pout. "What's a gal gotta do to get a rise out of you?"

He stared straight ahead, but the faintest tinge of a blush appeared on the crest of his cheekbones. She drew out the silence for an excruciatingly long, tense minute and a half before saying throatily, "Oh. *That.*"

She lifted her scarlet-tipped hand.

"Don't even think it," he warned, his lips barely moving.

Lacey's hand hovered above Alec's chest. Though the chill in his voice was off-putting, she'd never been one to be easily put off. Then again, she might be starting something she'd regret. But, no, she believed the credo that it is only what we *don't* do that we regret.

She placed her hand on Alec's chest and went up on her knees at the same time, so she could lean over him and touch her lips to his without risking *too* much of the kind of contact it might be difficult to pull away from. Through her palm she felt the intake of his breath, the expansion of his ribs and the firm, rounded band of muscles—*pectorals*, she thought dazedly—and then she was kissing him. Not a steamy, lusty, let's-do-it-on-the-floor kiss. Just a nice, sweet, good-night-sleep-tight one.

Or at least it was until Alec's lips softened and his tongue grazed her teeth, flicking ever so lightly against the tip of her own tongue. She lost her breath then, along with her good intentions and her balance. She sank against him, her breasts mounding against the firmness of his flexing pectorals. First thing tomorrow she was going to start a fan club for his pectorals.

Alec wrapped his hands around her upper arms. For a moment she thought he was going to pull her even closer; their kiss was deepening with a warm, liquid languor. Instead, shockingly, his grip tightened and he abruptly pushed her away.

"Quit it," he said. "I'm not interested."

Lacey wiped her mouth with the back of her hand. "You are such a hypocrite," she said without thinking, startling even herself. Alec's expression was combative, but she knew a good exit line when she blurted one. She stood and stuck her nose in the air and marched to her bedroom without looking back. If that was what he wanted, she'd show him the best *quit* he'd ever seen!

ALEC DIDN'T MOVE. Not even to flinch when she slammed the door. He didn't move because if he did he knew he couldn't trust his body to take him to the exit

instead of Lacey's bedroom. The next time he opened
that door it would have to be for recreational purposes
only. If he was any kind of bodyguard at all, that meant
there'd never be a next time, because it was much too
easy for him to imagine Lacey reclining among the pillows, her body all soft and round, her come-hither lips
saying his name like an invitation....

Which was why he still wasn't moving.

He tried not to think about Lacey kissing him. About
the willingness of her mouth or the fullness of her
breasts cupped in beige lace or the hot blue challenge
of her eyes. When that didn't work he tried not to think
about the way she walked, and talked, and laughed so
freely.

Which didn't work, either, so he reminded himself
that it was his job to see that she continued to do all
three, even if it was for the benefit of some other guy
long after Alec had returned to his lonely outpost in
Virginia.

He could do it. He just had to stay strong. If equating
Lacey with Cat Szako helped—even though he was beginning to wonder if Jericho had been right about the
resemblance being only superficial—then that's what
he would do. Hell, he'd once survived two months of
hundred-degree heat in a tiny stone cell in Lebanon; he
understood about all the little tricks a person could em-
ploy to keep his head straight under pressure.

Tricks that could take a strange twist and drive you
crazy as easily as they could keep you sane.

THE PROBLEM WITH GREAT exit lines was that you had to
stay exited for them to retain their effectiveness. Lacey
pulled on a knee-length nightshirt, worrying over how
she could gracefully reappear. For one thing, she still
didn't know if Alec intended to stay the night. Plus she

had to use the bathroom, and that meant walking out there right in front of him and having him watch her with those sharp, brown-black eyes of his discerning every twitch of her skin and longing in her heart.

She put her ear to the door, listening for movement. Even though Alec made as much noise as a snake slithering through the underbrush, she should at least hear the sound of the door closing on his departure.

Nothing. *Nothing, nothing, nothing,* she said to herself, clutching her abdomen as she leaned against the door. Alec Danieli was the first male she'd ever kissed who'd responded with a big fat nothing, and that included her grandpa with Alzheimer's and her cousin Jeanette's six-month-old baby boy.

Of course, that wasn't strictly true. Alec the Hypocrite had wanted her to think he felt nothing, but even if she'd watched their kissing scene from the cheapest, obstructed-view balcony seat, she'd have known otherwise.

Which was beside the point. She'd had a ringside seat—practically a lap-side seat. She knew that he'd returned her kiss. And she knew that he'd wanted to do a whole lot more, even if what he'd ultimately decided on had amounted to less than zero.

Lacey was seized with feminine outrage. He'd pushed her away! *Incredible!*

It was probably good that one of them had stopped, though. For a lot of reasons.

She just couldn't remember what any of them were.

ALEC WAS MEASURING the benefits of going back to his hotel—where there would be a dozen city blocks between him and temptation—against the pitiful lineup of cheap locks on Lacey's front door. If she hadn't gotten the latest letter, he probably could have risked leaving her alone for the night. He'd intended to. But now...

Lacey stalked out of the bedroom wearing a gauzy white nightshirt that covered only half of her showgirl legs and did nothing whatsoever to conceal the shape and movement of her hips and breasts. He watched with approval. She shot him a quelling look from beneath her lashes and went into the bathroom and shut the door.

He'd just made up his mind.

He was staying.

In the bathroom, Lacey smiled foamily around the toothbrush in her mouth. Every cell of her body was singing the same refrain: He was staying!

LACEY GAVE HIM SHEETS and a pillow and a blanket, and was very chaste about it except for the swing of her breasts beneath the billowy nightshirt when she tossed the pillow to him from her bedroom doorway. She probably wondered why he still hadn't moved from the love seat, but she didn't ask, just said a pleasant good-night and closed her bedroom door.

He listened for the snicking sound of a lock. None came, which was an invitation in itself...if he was so inclined.

Telling himself he wasn't, he definitely wasn't, Alec got to his feet and slowly made up his sorry bed. He walked the long way around the papier-mâché trees to get to the bathroom. There was no gingerbread, only chipped ceramic tiles and a water-stained tub and fluffy towels that smelled like Lacey.

He used his thumb to wipe a smear of her dark red lipstick from his bottom lip, then stared at the stain on his thumb like a lovestruck fool. He thought again of Lacey's walk, her talk, her laugh, the way she threw herself into life, damn the consequences. She was wonderful, and her legs were fantastic, and her smile was— He looked up and caught a glimpse of his own unguarded expression in the mirror. *Quit it*, he told his reflection. *This is the kind of sentimental claptrap that dulls your wits.* Duly chastised, he washed up as violently as if the soap and water were removing Lacey from his thoughts.

The attempt wasn't successful. As he left the bathroom he started wondering if she was lying awake listening to every move he made. Was she hoping he'd make one in her direction, or had she fallen asleep immediately—the way that people who were either too amoral or too self-satisfied to know they should have a guilty conscience always seemed to. He tried to insert Lacey into that equation and instead ended up with another mental image of her in bed, waiting for him with her legs stretched long and bare across the sheets. Each wiggle of her painted toenails was beckoning, making it very easy for Alec to convince himself that she was wholesomely sexy and up-front, not duplicitous and conniving like Cat, not at all....

HE'D LEFT THE BATHROOM seven minutes ago. She knew because she'd watched as each minute changed over on her digital clock.

Lacey told herself to give up. Alec must have settled in for the night, even though she hadn't heard as much as a squeak from the love seat. How he could have done so without making a sound—the love seat was old and creaky and much too short for him—was beyond her. But, then, how he could deny their explosive chemistry was beyond her, too. Maybe it had something to do with his military training.

She sighed, twisting to find a sleeping position that

wouldn't rub any of her sensitive body parts against each other. Her night was going to be as long and uncomfortable as Alec's unless one of them had the courage to do something about it.

She rose from the bed and walked to the door. She put her hand on it, listening, hoping, praying. She knew she could seduce Alec if she wanted to, and she did, she did, but did she want him for just one night or forever?

Forever?

The shock of that was enough to send her leaping back to bed.

ALEC HAD LOST TRACK of how long he'd been standing with his hand on the knob of her bedroom door. There'd been a moment when he could have sworn she was there on the other side, hesitating on tenterhooks of desire, as ripe and swollen with need as he, but that had most likely been wishful thinking.

He'd been trying to convince himself that making love to Lacey would be a mistake. In a professional capacity, if not otherwise. And as he'd already made that mistake once in his life, twice would be unforgivable.

But still worth it? he wondered.

Finally he released the knob and backed away, knowing full well that doing so was something he'd always regret.

Still, he had his tattered honor—even though he knew from experience it wouldn't keep him warm at night.

5

First he felt the satin of her thighs and then the seductive warmth between them, shielded only by a scrap of lace. Startled by her recklessness, he tried to pull his hand away. She clutched it tighter, pressing his palm up hard against herself until he surrendered with a muttered oath. Blatantly he probed her damp feminine heat. She shut her eyes and moaned, arching into the pressure, the pleasure, her skirt crushed at her waist.

"Feel," she said huskily, the vapor of her breath rising from her parted lips. "Feel what a woman I am."

He stroked her roughly, intimately, and the tremor that coursed through her reverberated on his fingertips. "It takes more than this," he said harshly, not liking himself for it. But she didn't know what she was asking for. And he didn't know if he wanted to be the one to shatter her pretty illusions. He took his hand away, the icy air a shock on his exposed skin.

She measured his response in silence. "Then show me," she said at last, with a sassy flip of her red curls. She smoothed down her skirt, lashes lowering invitingly. "Come upstairs, Daniels, and show me everything."

"THEN THIS MORNING he acted as though nothing had happened between us," Lacey said. She pointed out a wig to the salesgirl. "Except for being a teensy bit friendlier. He even made pancakes for breakfast—like my hips needed pancakes. I, of course, was too polite not to eat them."

"You kissed him," Amalie said, a couple of beats behind. "I can't believe you kissed him. Just like that."

Lacey pinned up her hair and slipped on the long, curly red wig. "How'd you kiss Jericho the first time? If someone doesn't do it—just like that—who's to say it ever gets done?"

"We kissed in the back seat of a cab," Amalie murmured. "And it was devastating. I was in his lap before I—" She shook her head, smiling. "But I digress."

"Hmm. I wouldn't say that Alec's kiss was exactly devastating. The world didn't shake. It was nice, though." *Extremely nice.* "It had potential." *Genius potential.*

"But he's your bodyguard," Amalie said. "Ethically, it may not be the proper thing to do. And professionally…well, do you really want your bodyguard to be quite that distracted?"

"Aw, c'mon, Am. Have you forgotten that Jericho was a journalist writing a story about *Black Velvet* and Madame X when you two got together? If you want to talk questionable ethics…"

Amalie flushed. "You're right, of course. I guess I think of Jericho and myself as an exception to the rule."

Lacey laughed and patted the flamboyant red curls. "I'm exceptional, too, sweetie."

"And Alec?"

Lacey's gaze skipped past the multitude of department store wigs and picked out one black, shaggy head and one a sandy blond. The men were conferring again. Coming up with a plan that would put the breaks on her career, no doubt. "To be honest, I'm not sure what Alec is, other than a mystery." She sighed and tugged the wig lower over her hairline. "What do you think?"

Amalie tilted her head to one side. "The wig is…exceptional. In its way. As for Alec, well…"

Lacey stopped fussing with the wild red curls. "Aha. You know something. I suspected as much." Her curiosity was by now so heightened that she became impatient with Amalie's hesitation. "Tell me, tell me," she coaxed. "Pretty please."

Amalie bit her lip. "Jericho didn't say it was a secret. Still, I—"

"He's my bodyguard. We're living this close." Holding up her crossed fingers, Lacey checked on the men again. They were out of earshot. "I ought to know everything there is to know about him."

"It's a matter of public record," Amalie conceded. "It happened in Zhabekistan nearly two years ago. Do you remember the scandal at their American embassy?"

"Wait a minute. Zhabekistan is one of those tiny countries that split from the Soviet Union, am I right? What was Alec doing there?"

"He was supposedly in charge of embassy security, but Jericho hinted that there might have been something shady about Alec's assignment. Jericho never found out the specifics. Anyway, what happened was that some of the embassy guards were court-martialed for associating with a spy. The Mata Hari of the Mideast, the press dubbed her. The guards had revealed confidential information to her that led to an attack on the embassy by Zhabekistani rebels who, in turn, had been covertly funded by the Iranians. Jericho was there. He wrote a series of articles about the whole tangled mess. He was nominated for a Pulitzer Prize."

Aha! Lacey thought of Alec's odd reaction when she'd blundered onto the subject with her joke about spy school. So that was why... "What was Alec's involvement?" she asked quickly. "He wasn't..." She knew he wasn't. He couldn't be.

"No," Amalie said. "Well, I guess he was under suspicion for a while, but he was cleared once everything was sorted out. Jericho said that after all the scandal and notoriety, though, Alec felt that he had to resign his commission. He disappeared from public view."

"I do remember the heated talk about those embassy guards," Lacey murmured. "There are few things this country reviles more than a traitor."

"I wouldn't even *think* that word around Alec. He's likely to be touchy about—"

"Shh," Lacey cautioned. "They're coming this way."

Amalie looked alarmed. "Seriously, Lacey. This isn't a subject to be taken lightly."

"Give me some credit." Lacey jammed a curly blond afro onto her head. "My mouth isn't that big, even if it sometimes seems like it."

"You've never been known for your discretion," Amalie whispered worriedly. "Please don't say—"

"Hiya, guys!" Lacey aimed a cheerful smile past Amalie's shoulder. "Whaddya think?"

"I think you two have been gossiping as if this was a back fence, not a sales counter." Jericho looked suspiciously from Lacey's bright eyes to his wife's pink cheeks.

"And I think you look like a gothic Shirley Temple," said Alec. "Which is not quite the unobtrusive image we're after."

Lacey was still digesting her new information about

Alec. She wanted to stare into his austere face until she knew him to the depths of his soul, but that would probably be considered inappropriate behavior. Instead she conjured up a tame smile and looked down at her leather pants and black velvet tunic hung with heavy chains and a baroque cross. Unfortunately, Alec was right. "Then I imagine you won't like the red curly wig, either."

He dismissed it with a lift of his eyebrows.

"I told her to try the brunette shag," Amalie interjected.

"Yechh," Lacey drawled, then winced when she glanced at her friend's short, dark coif. "No offense, Am. You suit the Audrey Hepburn look. I'm more a stretched-out Marilyn Monroe. With the smile to match."

"We'll try the brown one," Jericho said to the salesclerk.

Lacey tilted her chin at him. "And I'm sure *we'll* look lovely."

He took the wig from the clerk and plopped it on Lacey's head. "Perfect. We'll take it."

She opened her mouth to make a token protest and he put her off by handing her a pair of wire-framed sunglasses with pale brown lenses. "Try these."

After snugging the wig in place and tucking away stray strands of her hair, she slipped on the glasses and turned reluctantly to the round mirror set up on the counter. "Wow. Check me out. No more Madame X. In fact, I look kind of like—"

"Me," said Amalie with an astonished giggle. "This is weird. First I was you, or should I say you were me, on the *Black Velvet* book tour. And now..." She took a tissue and wiped away Lacey's red lipstick. "Yup, that does it. You're me."

"Jericho, was this your idea?" Lacey asked in an accusing tone. "Are you getting revenge on us for tricking you into believing I was Madame X aka Amalie Dove?"

"Turnabout is fair play," he said with a grin. Amalie clamped her hand over her mouth and leaned against him, her shoulders shaking as she tried not to laugh at Lacey's abrupt transformation.

"Okay, it's amusing, I'll give you that." Lacey peered into the mirror, disconcerted. "But is it wise? Do we want my secret admirer to mistake me for Amalie? Maybe I should go for the red wig instead."

"No," Alec said. "The thing is to avoid any appearance that might attract Mr. X's notice." He indicated the nondescript wig. "You'll blend into the crowd in this wig—"

"That's what I'm afraid of," Lacey muttered.

"—but no one would ever mistake you for Amalie." His glance skated down Lacey's body. "Not when you're still six feet tall and shaped more like Countess Pushkin than a tomboy—"

Lacey interrupted. "Amalie, do you want to kick him or shall I?"

Amalie set her hands on her slender hips and evaluated Alec's apparent transgression. "Well, I *was* once a tomboy...."

"And at least he compared me to the countess and not, say, a big fat lady opera singer." Lacey pulled off the wig and glasses and gave Alec a warning look. "We're going to leave your vital body parts intact this time. Just watch your step. I don't take kindly to—"

"Keep talking," Alec said in a low voice. She thought he was being sarcastic until she saw his expression. "Act natural," he added automatically, his eyes searching the aisles of the department store. "Both of you."

Lacey started to turn to see what he was looking for. "What—"

Alec pushed her onto a stool and rolled her up to the counter. He grabbed the red wig off its stand and slapped it on her head. "For once, just do what I say."

Jericho armed Amalie with a hairbrush. "Stay right here, sweetheart. You'll be okay."

Before either woman could react, Alec and Jericho sauntered away, looking exactly like men bored with shopping—except for the rigid set of their shoulders and the intensity radiating from their narrowed eyes.

"DO YOU SEE HIM?" Jericho said under his breath.

Alec paused beside a display of purses and pretended to examine them as he obliquely searched for the suspicious man who'd been lurking on the other side of the wig counter. "He went over there, toward the gloves. I think he's circling around toward the wigs again."

They glanced back at the women. Amalie was brushing Lacey's wig. Lacey was talking fast, her eyes darting around the store. She kept trying to stand; every time she did Amalie pushed down on her shoulders until she sat again. They looked anything but natural.

"We'd better try to corner him," Jericho said. "I'll go this way."

Alec doubled back and strolled past the wig display. Lacey and Amalie watched with wide eyes; when Lacey's mouth opened he put a finger to his in a hushing motion. She sank lower on the stool, her lips clamped shut, her eyes as electric as the wild red wig.

Alec caught a colorful flurry of movement out of the corner of his eye. A rack of silk scarves shuddered as he approached. Jericho appeared from the other direction and Alec pointed to the pair of feet sidling past the chrome display stand.

Suddenly a thin blond man shot out from behind the rack, trailing multicolored scarves like a magician's pocket. "Grab him!" Jericho said. Alec lunged, but came up with only a handful of a fringed lace shawl.

"Heads up," he called to warn the women as the man careened toward them, arms pinwheeling. Lacey jumped up and shot the heavy chrome stool into the aisle. There was a crash and a howl of pain.

Alec arrived in time to close his hand on the back of the guy's neck and jerk him to his feet. "Who are you?"

The stalker writhed, keening incoherently as he clawed at the vise at his throat. Alec bent one of the man's arms behind his back, holding him still so they could all get a good look at him. Pale and blond, skinny as a pencil, dressed in Dockers and an argyle sweater, the guy appeared to be as meek a stalker as one could wish for.

"Malcolm?" Amalie said with a quaver.

Jericho stared at her. "You know him?"

"It's Malcolm," she said with relief. "Oh, Alec, let him go. You're hurting him."

Alec eased his grip by one or two degrees. Just because the guy was a dweeb didn't mean his fantasies about Madame X hadn't taken a dangerous turn. "Do you recognize him, Lacey?"

She pushed back the red wig that had slipped sideways over one eye. "I don't think so," she said doubtfully, and Malcolm's concave chest heaved with a deep sigh of longing. Hanging limply in Alec's grasp, he gazed at Lacey with glazed eyes, his chin trembling.

"Sure you do." Amalie stepped forward and patted

Malcolm's shoulder. "He goes to all the area *Black Velvet* events. We've both signed books for him."

"I—I don't remember."

"Do we have a problem here, sir?" asked a store security guard.

"Not anymore," Alec said, "but you can do me a favor and call the police."

"You didn't have to do that," Amalie protested, while Alec dispatched the guard. "I know Malcolm, I've talked to him many times. He's harmless. Just a fan."

"I'm Madame X's biggest fan," Malcolm said cravenly.

Alec snorted and slipped the captive's wallet from his pocket. "Malcolm O'Brian," he read from the ID inside. "Brooklyn, New York." Alec gave Malcolm's arm a little jog, and though the fellow yipped in alarm, his eyes didn't swerve from Lacey. "You might think up a better fake name the next time you send a lady your underwear," Alec hissed into Malcolm's ear.

"Malcolm didn't write the letters." Amalie's face was crimped with concern. "I'm sure of it."

"Fine, but let's proceed with caution," said Jericho. He exchanged a look with Alec; neither man was as quick to dismiss their suspect as sweet-natured Amalie.

Alec considered Lacey. Still wearing the red wig, she was leaning against the counter on her elbows, one long, black-leather-covered leg crossed over the other. She didn't look convinced, either, but neither did she seem afraid. Of course, he thought, *she* wouldn't.

"What do you say, Lacey?" he prompted.

She shook her head. "I don't know him. But he doesn't look threatening to me. I think it's safe to let go of his arm before you snap it in two."

Alec patted down the guy for weapons, then released him. Malcolm took a wobbling step toward Lacey before the look in Alec's eye brought him up short. "You're Madame X," he said, almost panting as his eyes gobbled her up. "I can't believe I'm this close to Madame X." He put out his hand, then withdrew it as unworthy. "You're a *goddess.*"

Lacey brightened, and removed the red wig with a flourish. "Y'all gave us a scare, Malcolm." With a friendly smile, she shook her blond mane loose across her shoulders. "Next time, darlin', just walk up and introduce yourself."

Malcolm made a yearning sound in his throat, a sound that might have prompted Alec to pop the guy one if he hadn't almost produced the same sound himself last night outside Lacey's bedroom door. Man, what a sap he'd been, nearly as cracked a case as Malcolm.

"Why were you following us?" Alec asked, although the answer was evident.

Malcolm simpered. "I only wanted to meet Madame X."

Alec's voice came out even deeper and gruffer in response. "You sure that's all?"

Jericho was equally suspicious. "And how did you know where she'd be?"

Malcolm took a folded newspaper clipping from his wallet. "It said so in the *Express.* Seven o'clock at the Paramus mall with the rest of the cast of *All That Glitters.* Madame X will give out free autographed Velvet Valancy pictures."

"Right," Alec said; he'd also made himself familiar with Lacey's itinerary. "One problem, though, O'Brian. This isn't Paramus."

Malcolm's face became washed with color. "I, uh, I, uh…"

"Here come the cops," the security guard announced.

"Don't worry." Amalie soothed Malcolm, who was quaking in his tasseled loafers. "You may have to answer a few questions, but I'll vouch for you."

Lacey frowned. "Alec? Do we have to turn him in to the police?"

Alec couldn't believe his ears. *Save me from softhearted women*, he thought in disgust, even while saying very mildly, "Just doing my job, Ms. Longwood."

Lacey glowered, but he wouldn't reconsider. Out of some fathomless motivation, she relented with a flutter of her lashes, putting a teasing hand on his arm as she brushed past him in her swingy velvet top on her way to console Malcolm on his impending arrest. "You're an awfully nasty man, Mr. Danieli," she said softly, using her throaty voice to full advantage as for a fleeting moment she pressed herself against him. "A real tough nut."

Alec held himself very still until she'd passed. *Save me from just plain soft women, too*, he added silently, even though it was no use. He already had it worse than Malcolm.

ALEC HANDED Malcolm O'Brian over to the city police. Lurking in a department store wasn't illegal, so the cops could only detain him for questioning by the detective who was familiar with the case. Alec wasn't optimistic that the identity and motives of Madame X's mystery date would result from the cursory investigation. Like everyone else, he'd come to doubt that Malcolm was the author of the offensive letters—the man was a sycophant, not a psychopath.

Pointedly, Lacey brushed off the incident as a typical hysterical-male overreaction on Alec's part. And she insisted that they proceed as planned with the scheduled publicity event for *All That Glitters*.

Late that afternoon, Amalie and Jericho departed for South Carolina, with Amalie still swearing that Malcolm was a timid soul who meant no harm. It had turned out that she alone had spoken to him several times at book signings, as he'd been too awestruck to approach the goddess that was Madame X for anything more than an autograph. Lacey laughed and said that she'd always wanted to have men worshipping at her feet, and Alec snorted and said that while goddesses were immortal, flesh-and-blood women weren't, and, furthermore, she might want to reconsider encouraging all the foot fetishists out there. They sparred from the hotel elevator to the front desk to the airport shuttle parked at the curb. Amalie and Lacey hugged goodbye. Jericho slapped Alec between the shoulder blades in wordless thanks, encouragement...and commiseration.

Ninety minutes later, Alec escorted the goddess to Paramus.

Having nothing to do but stand and watch and think, he found that his mind began taking strange turns. *The Goddess of Hot Fudge Sundaes*, he mentally dubbed Lacey as she was introduced to a crowd of enthusiastic soap opera fans. Wearing another of the signature black velvet outfits, she bopped over to the microphone to say a few words, then stepped back to join the rest of the cast, waving both hands overhead as she spun on the spike-heeled boots that made her tower over most of the actors. Including, to Alec's secret amusement, the "hunk" with an unbuttoned shirt who was plenty large on the small screen, but no more than five-seven in real life.

Restlessly, Alec scanned the crush around the stage, searching over and over for the man who would be Mr. X. He could be tall, short, round, furtive or cocky. He could look like Lars Torberg, like Malcolm O'Brian, like a wild-eyed psychopath. There was no telling.

Again Lacey drew Alec's eye. She was incandescent, lit up like the Fourth of July, basking in attention as she greeted fans and passed out publicity photos. It wasn't merely a matter of ego gratification, he saw. She was genuinely enjoying herself, managing to make a quick personal contact with each person who approached her by patting arms, clasping hands, even getting down on her haunches to greet children face-to-face. Under the circumstances it wasn't the wisest method of operation, but by now Alec knew that telling Lacey to be less personable would be like telling a canary not to sing.

She would be what she would be. Joyful, outlandish, indulgent, alarming. Giving, taking, laughing, loving.

The Goddess of Hot Fudge Sundaes.

And all I want is a taste, he thought. *Just one taste.*

ALEC WENT TO TALK with Lil Wingo, a photographer with an eloquent eye and a limited vocabulary. He knew her from his months in Zhabekistan, when she'd paired with Jericho to cover the embassy spy scandal. Alec's relationship with Lil had been, at times, adversarial; she'd sold several shots to the wire services of the besieged Lieutenant Colonel Danieli in his dress blues.

Alec indicated the cavorting actors and shrieking crowd. "I'm surprised to see you here."

Lil aimed her camera. "Paying the rent," she said,

and focused on a large woman who was hugging "Case" so enthusiastically she'd lifted him off the ground. "Editors prefer celebrities to wars these days."

Alec knew it was so. One of the reasons the Zhabek-istan story had received so much play was because Cat Szako, the exotic blond spy, had made it "sexy" and "salable."

"And you?" Lil said, giving him a quick once-over from beneath dark brown bangs. In boots, worn suede pants and a floppy safari jacket, she looked lean and tough, as though she'd been cured in the sun. Perhaps she had, Alec thought, remembering the relentless sun and barren, rocky coast of Zhabekistan.

At her speculative look, Alec worried that she'd turn her camera on him. But, no, he realized. He was old news. Once he'd been proven innocent, and thus dull, his notoriety had faded. Eventually his name would be downgraded to footnote status.

"Payback," he said, as terse as Lil.

She grunted and mumbled, "Jericho." That was all.

Alec waited five minutes before he spoke again. "You've shot a lot of film of Madame X over the past few months?"

"Yep."

He thought it might prove interesting to get his hands on her backlog of photos. See who showed up among Madame X's admirers. How to get Lil to turn them over without revealing his reasons would be a delicate operation. He didn't want the ultrasalable story of Madame X's obsessed fan getting out to the press. However, if Lil was still loyal to Jericho, Alec could likely persuade her to cooperate.

"She's real popular," Lil volunteered, prowling around the edges of the crowd until she had a good angle on Lacey. Alec followed. "Photogenic," Lil continued, snapping away. "Money in the bank."

"You've got a sharp eye."

Lil grunted.

"Have you noticed anyone in particular at the *Black Velvet* events?"

She straightened and gave him her whole attention. "Whaddya mean?"

Alec avoided her deep stare. "You know. A…an especially *interested* bystander."

Face squeezed with thought, she peered at him with one eye squinted almost shut. She poked her tongue into her cheek. "Why was it that you're here again?"

"I'm Lacey Longwood's bodyguard," he said reluctantly, although there was no reason not to admit it. Judging by the number of dark glasses and earphones on the men ostentatiously hovering near their clients, this set of actors hired bodyguards as commonly as personal trainers.

"Ah, I see." Lil's Popeye expression evened out. Her gaze turned to Lacey, who looked up and smiled her great, beaming smile for the camera. Lil clicked off one token frame. "Are you making general inquiries or referring to someone specific? You got some trouble?"

"Just being thorough." All of Alec's protective instincts were on guard, flooding him with memories of what it had been like to be hounded by the press. Not for anything would he go through that again, he vowed. Not for Jericho. Not for Lacey.

Not even for Lacey, he silently repeated, making it as convincing as he could.

Lil grunted again. "Madame X has got her zealous admirers, that's for damn sure."

"But would you say there's any one in particular I should watch out for?"

With a wry chuckle, Lil readjusted the strap of her camera against her frayed collar. "The way I figure it, between grabby fans, pushy publicists and sharky agents, Madame X is gonna someday wake up to find herself ground up like a side of beef."

Alec's brows lifted. "You forgot to mention obtrusive photographers."

Lil shrugged, not taking offense. "I'm just a chronicler of the times, yada, yada, yada."

He wasn't going to argue the point. "So…have you chronicled anything incriminating lately?"

"As far as Madame X goes?"

"Yes."

"'Course not," Lil said gruffly, turning away to pack up her camera equipment.

"Right. Because if you had, the pictures would have been in the tabloids by now," Alec observed.

Although Lil shrugged again, her thoughtful, measuring expression as she rewound her film made Alec decide that he would definitely speak to Jericho about approaching her to turn over her file of Madame X photos. "Keep an eye out for me, will you?" he asked casually. "Just in case."

"Sure." Lil saluted and hoisted her camera bag. "Eyes open, lens cap off."

"I expected no less."

ALEC ESCORTED LACEY to the mall's rest rooms so she could change out of her black velvet and into… "Sackcloth and ashes," she said under her breath, following him into the ladies' room. He'd announced his impending invasion at the door, and several women had already bolted. A third was hiding out in the only occupied stall.

Alec crouched to examine a pair of feet clad in

chunky, toes-in oxfords. "Ma'am, I'm going to have to ask you to show yourself."

Lacey heaved her duffel bag onto the ledge above the sinks. "Alec, c'mon. She's not Mr. X. I'm perfectly safe. Go and guard the door like a good li'l marine."

He stood abruptly, his posture ramrod straight. "Just being thorough, Ms. Longwood."

One tiny slip of the tongue and he reverted to type, she noted. Well, according to Grandma Lacey-Beth, there was more than one way to skin a banana. "And I appreciate it, sweetie, really I do." Lacey turned her back to him and lifted her hair off her neck. She wiggled her shoulders, which were bare beneath the smoky layer of illusion fabric that formed the sleeves and upper bodice of her clingy dress. "Since you're staying, would you unzip me?"

Alec hesitated, as she'd known he would.

The stall banged open and a pasty-skinned Fiona Apple look-alike came out. The sullen teen glared at Alec, took one last defiant drag on her cigarette and stopped on her way out of the rest room to unzip Lacey down to the waistband of her panty hose.

Lacey held her hair up for a moment longer so Alec could get an eyeful of her long, bare back. He looked. And when he came back to himself, he departed apace.

"Girl power," Lacey said to the empty bathroom.

She stripped out of her glam rags and pulled on the various pieces of her anti–Madame X costume. First, gray woolen tights that looked like long underwear. Then another ex-roomie leftover, a long, loose print shift that was about as flattering as her country grandma's faded housedresses. A pair of thick-soled, lace-up ankle boots. The drab wig, the dreary glasses and, after a quick wash with soap and water, no makeup at all. Lacey grimaced at herself as she stuck her arms into Alec's contribution to her metamorphosis, a bulky, khaki, hooded sweat jacket that was meant to further camouflage her figure.

When she zipped it up, she no longer looked like Amalie. She looked like a nearsighted Laura Ashley commando on a bad-hair day. Her bodyguard was going to love it.

Two big-haired women entered the rest room on a wave of cigarette smoke and Chanel No. 5. "Gawd!" said one of them in a raspy voice. "If I had a man like that I wouldn't leave him waiting outside the ladies', easy pickin's for every Tina who wiggles by." She eyed Lacey doubtfully. "He's not yours, is he, honey?"

Lacey threw her velvet dress, nylons and boots into the duffel. "I'm afraid so."

"Listen, honey, I'm gonna give ya some advice. *Free makeovers at the cosmetics counter in Saks.*" A wave of the woman's cigarette was followed by a hacking cough. "And that's all I'm gonna say."

Lacey looked at her reflection. *Yechh.* "Gee," she said, "maybe I'll do that."

The other woman chimed in with further encouragement as Lacey exited. "With a little effort you could be real pretty!"

Lacey peeked outside and saw that Alec was indeed waiting right beside the door. She slipped from the rest room, sidled up next to him and spoke low in his ear. "How'd you know Mr. X isn't a cross-dresser? One of those women you just let in could have pulled a—"

He whipped his head around. "Lacey, haven't I asked you not to treat this as a joke?"

"Pulled a curling wand," she concluded, ignoring his question. She thrust the duffel bag into his midsection as if it was a medicine ball. "They thought I needed a makeover."

"You look fine for our purposes."

Stepping out to the center of the corridor, she danced under the fluorescent lights, holding out her skirt and twirling round and round, rising to the toes of her boots. "I feel pretty, oh, so pretty...."

"Knock it off." Alec caught one of her arms when she started prancing toward the main concourse of the mall. He pulled her toward him, restraining her exuberance. "Don't move like that. You're drawing attention to yourself."

She rolled her eyes, but the feel of his hard, lean body pressed against her was enough to deal with— she didn't need his sniping, too. She walked on more sedately.

He stopped to consider her transformation. "Don't swing your hips. And try to slouch a little."

She swung her arms instead, like a gorilla, clumping her feet in the heavy boots, her head pulled forward between hunched shoulders. Alec stood watching and shaking his head, trying to look intolerant of her high jinks.

She gestured for him to join her, making a goofy face at his reluctance. "C'mon, Pa," she said. "Reckon it's time fer us to leave this durn city. We gotta get back to the farm and shoot us some critters, Pa."

He came. "I might as well have let you parade through the mall in a black velvet bikini. You're determined to make a spectacle of yourself either way."

"It's in my nature," she said airily.

Still, she tried to behave herself as they left the mall and eventually New Jersey, crossing the Hudson into Manhattan in Alec's GM pickup. She was surprised that he drove a pickup, of all vehicles. A silver or black sports car seemed more along his lines, something stylish and racy, but understated. Certainly not a teal-colored pickup with bales of straw and a crusty pitch-fork in the back.

She asked him about the straw.

He didn't answer right away. She decided that he was scowling at the Upper West Side traffic, not at her question. In fact, aside from the scowl—and New York traffic was bad enough to make the pope scowl—Alec appeared more relaxed than he had since she'd known him. He'd stopped checking the rearview mirror for suspicious headlights. Nor were his eyes continually straying in her direction, as they had when the sight of her in black velvet had apparently caused him such pain.

The double-parked delivery truck that had been holding up traffic finally moved on, to a typical jeering, honking, sarcastic salute from other drivers. Alec shifted gears and said, "After a year and a half in the country, I'm not used to city traffic."

"Oh?"

As they circled her block, looking for a parking space on the crowded, dirty streets, he told her about his place in Virginia, where he raised horses in peace and quiet and fresh air. He laughed when that reminded her of being twelve years old and trying to ride bare-back on her country grandma's swaybacked mare and falling off into the muddy corral wearing a fringed, white suede cowgirl costume. To entertain this new, looser Alec, she made the story sound funnier than it had actually played out—her mother had cried over the ruination of the pricey pageant costume, and Lacey had felt so bad she'd gone another year before confessing that she'd been wanting to quit pageants to sing lead for her preteen girlfriends' garage band, the Pogos.

Finally Alec found a spot two blocks from Lacey's

apartment. It was late, she was hungry and tired and her scalp was itching like the dickens, but suddenly she didn't want to leave the cozy space of the pickup cab. She looked over at Alec, fascinated that he'd entranced her with no effort at all when other men had to continually strive to keep her entertained.

Alec was drumming his fingers on the steering wheel, reflections of flickering city lights sliding across his contemplative face. She looked away, her mouth gone dry with yearning.

Finally she had to speak, even though her voice came out all sandpapery. "You like me better this way, don't you?"

Alec tensed. "Not necessarily."

"Then how come this is the first time we've been having an actual conversation instead of a battle of wills?"

"Uh…"

"Why do you respond better to me when I don't look like myself?" she wondered out loud, not actually expecting him to answer. The question was directed mainly to herself. She plucked at the pastel, flower-patterned dress; maybe it wasn't *so* ugly.

"It's not you," he said, looking uncomfortable with her again. That, she regretted. "I mean, it's not your appearance."

Her eyes fastened on him. "Oh, yeah?"

Alec stared past the windshield at the late-night parade of assorted kooks, sophisticates, tourists and low-lifes. "Okay, so maybe the Madame X look isn't…" He searched for words. "You're too…"

"Obvious?" she suggested, with more regret. Far from being the basic-issue marine she'd expected, Alec was a man of layers, of subtleties. It followed that his taste in women would be as discriminating.

"Not exactly," he said.

"Overpowering?"

"Of course not."

"Then what is it, Alec? Why…" She pressed her lips together. *Stop asking. This isn't a pageant; Alec's not your judge. You don't have to captivate every man you meet.* She glanced out at the stream of traffic with glimmering eyes. "Hey, you know what? We should stop off at Big Zito's for a couple of whopping deli sandwiches. They have great pie, too."

Her sally didn't work, and she couldn't think of anything else to say. She and Alec fell into a silence so deep she couldn't touch bottom.

After a while she couldn't sit still, either. She shifted position, holding her breath, tucking her hands into tight fists so she wouldn't reach out for Alec and drown them both with the enormity of her growing desires.

Finally he turned his dark, liquid eyes on her, and she heard his soft voice coming toward her from far away. "You are beautiful, Lacey."

She still didn't dare to breathe. But he hadn't sounded grudging or insincere. He'd sounded… significant.

And Lacey realized that for maybe the first time in her life, she didn't want to captivate every man she met.

Only Alec.

6

Daniels followed Laryssa into the manor house.

She was charged with erotic daring. The lingering effects of his crude, elemental caress were making her vibrate inside like a tuning fork. How long had she anticipated this? How long had she wanted him naked inside her, so deep and hard and strong that there would be no turning back...ever?

The entrance hall was vast and quiet, the thick wool carpet and mahogany wainscoting absorbing every sound except the sonorous gong of the stately grandfather clock. To the right a small fire was lit in the library fireplace, but Laryssa craved privacy far more than warmth. Fortunately, with Daniels, she could have both.

She swept up the long, curving stairway without glancing back. She knew he was following her—she could feel his eyes trained on her swaying hips.

THE DOORMAN at Lacey's building didn't go off shift until early morning, so he was still in the wainscoted lobby when she and Alec came through the doors in such a rush he didn't have time to usher them through. His head bobbed. "Good evening, Miss, er... Longwood? Mr. Danieli."

"Yes, it's true, it's me," Lacey said, removing the

glasses. Laughing at Alec with her eyes, she did her clomping farmer's walk to the elevators. "You see," she accused when the doors slid shut, "the doorman recognized me even in costume."

"Only just."

She peeled back the wig and tore the pins from her hair. "Ah, yes, free at last." Catching Alec's eye as she dug her fingernails into her itchy scalp, she said, "Don't look at me like that. You don't know." She scratched vigorously. "You have no idea what tortures women go through to look beautiful."

"Most of it's unnecessary." He punched in her floor number.

"Says you." *And he had*, she thought with real warmth. He'd said she was beautiful—even though she'd been wearing the wig and glasses.

But wait a second. What if that meant he really *did* like her better in costume? Surely not! No man in his right mind would prefer the anti–Madame X, even one as stoic and reserved and averse to flamboyance as her bodyguard.

Then again, after just one look, Jericho had lost his heart to pretty-but-subdued Amalie, not Lacey-as-Madame X. Lacey knew that Amalie and Jericho's kind of love—the honest, everlasting kind—wasn't built on something as superficial as an attraction to blond hair and big boobs, even with a host of *Black Velvet* fantasies backing them up.

Which didn't bode well for Lacey's immediate love life. Depending, of course, on what Alec had meant when he said she was beautiful. Was there a discreet, unconceited way to ask?

Nervously she raked her fingers through her hair. When Alec glanced at her, his look seemed to convey more meaning than usual. She leaned against the elevator doors and took a steadying breath to counteract the intoxication of the sexual daring drumming through her veins. *Go on and ask him*, she challenged herself, *just like that*. After all, she was not—and never had been—the bashful type.

The question came out a whisper, nonetheless. "Am I beautiful enough to kiss?"

Alec said, "Pardon?" and put his hands out as the creaky old elevator lurched to a start and began its slow, shuddering ascent to the sixth floor.

"I said…" She took his hand and placed it over her heart. "Am I beautiful enough to kiss?"

He steadied himself, his fingers reaching fractionally for the swell of her breast. "You know you are." He stepped closer, his hand definitely sliding lower, his black lashes lowering, too, as his brooding gaze fastened on her mouth.

He took his time. Lacey's anticipation ballooned until waiting for Alec's kiss was her entire world. Wanting him filled her mind, her heart, her body, until vaguely she realized that this wasn't a good sign for the future, having one little kiss mean so much, not a good sign at all. Still, she couldn't bring herself to worry about tomorrow when the present was so engaging.

She was dimly aware of the doors vibrating against her spine as the elevator slowed.

Hurry up, she said silently to Alec, her head tilting back in offering, though for once she knew better than to kiss him first despite the hot, breathless, prickly frustration of waiting for him to make up his mind. *Hurry up!*

Just as Alec's lips found hers, the doors gave a warning *bing* and started to open. Lost in the kiss, she couldn't have cared less if she landed on her backside in the hallway—as long as Alec came with her—but he had the presence of mind to wind one arm around her waist to help her keep her balance.

The doors closed again. Alec gave a low moan and thrust against her, not gently, pushing her half up against the doors, half against the control panel. The elevator car jogged once and resumed its endless journey. Neither noticed. They were consumed by their kiss, their rapacious, intemperate, openmouthed kiss.

It was so overwhelming and went on for so long that they were still locked together—lips sliding, tongues sucking, fingers fumbling with clumsy caresses—when the elevator opened onto the lobby. Slowly Alec raised his eyes to the doorman's dumbstruck face, then slammed the flat of his hand against the control panel. Not thinking, not caring, he climbed back inside the wild roller-coaster ride of their kiss even before the doors closed.

Lacey rocked forward on the balls of her feet, her mouth hot on Alec's, her fingers twined around the lapels of his tweed jacket as all her weight slumped into him, knocking them both into the opposite corner of the car like the careening pellets of a pinball machine. Alec swiveled, his hands riding low on her hips, and pushed her flat against the wall, pinning her with one thrust of his thigh. She opened her mouth, drinking him in, tasting their mutual need, her legs so weak she slumped bonelessly against the paneling until all that kept her upright were her arms braced on the handrail and the saddle of Alec's thigh, and Alec's hands clasping her face, lifting it to his lips. The low rumbling vibration of the elevator seemed a part of their hunger as they kept kissing, kissing, kissing….

It was wonderful. It was delicious. It was crazy.

The doors gave another *bing*. Lacey opened her eyes

wide to meet Alec's, and their kiss turned into a smothered laugh and back into a kiss as she slowly straightened her knees, sliding higher with both hands pressing against his shoulders for leverage. Toe-to-toe, they continued kissing, gone quiet and staring into each other's eyes. After the frantic deluge, it was strangely touching, almost—but not quite—sobering.

The doors started to close, and finally the two of them broke apart and fell from the elevator, staggering along the hallway like tipsy party goers. Lacey looked at the apartment doors and put her hand to her hair in confusion. "We're on the tenth floor," she said, stunned, but beginning again to laugh.

Alec didn't because suddenly his throat was too tight. This was something he'd never known, this wild, laughing, joyous tumble into ecstasy. He wondered if it was always that way with Lacey.

"Not the elevator," he said when she turned toward it.

She gave him an arch look, murmured, "If you insist," and led him to the narrow, twisting stairway. They raced down four flights, their footsteps clattering and Lacey's exuberant laugh echoing through the stairwell every time she eluded his grasp. She leaped into space from midway down the final flight, and his heart stopped for an instant as she fell, her dress and hair billowing, then hit the floor with a flat-footed thud and sprang up as neatly as a cat.

"C'mon," she said, pushing through the unlatched fire door. "Hurry up."

He wanted to, very much. His pulse was a drumbeat in his ears, his desire reduced to primal instinct. And still he hesitated.

"Alec?" she said, holding the door open and looking up at him standing in the shadowed stairwell.

He descended slowly. "We need to have a serious talk."

She slammed into the hallway. "Please don't do this to me now."

Something burst inside him. "Do you think I don't want you? Do you think I wouldn't like to go inside and take you naked and laughing on the bed with your hair spread out and your mouth open and your breasts—your breasts..." He stopped, shocked, heart pounding, lungs seized up until Lacey came over, twining her arms around his waist, and he found he could breathe again. With his head tilted back, he swallowed hard and made himself relax, even though there was still this terrible need gnawing at him from the inside out. He put his arms around Lacey and she made a small cooing sound and burrowed into him, her lips pressing soft damp kisses on his jaw and neck and ear. Suddenly he found himself speaking hoarsely into the gold silk of her hair, unable to hold back the rush of words for another second. "Your magnificent breasts, your innocent eyes, your smile, your sheer joy, your legs, oh, *man*, your long legs—I want all of you, Lacey, you fool, you beautiful fool...."

And even as his confession poured out he was wondering who was the fool—her for being so open and trusting, or him for being too thunderstruck by her vivid presence to think straight?

"Then what's the holdup?" she asked, insouciant. "We seem to be in agreement."

He scrambled for reasons to stop. He knew there were many. His honor? *Already ripped to shreds.* Her reputation as Madame X? *They'd only be fulfilling it.* His distrust? *As long as he didn't lose it...* The job? Yeah. *The job.*

"Lacey." He couldn't remember moving along the

hallway to her apartment door, but here they were. She put her key in the lock. "Lacey," he said desperately. "I have to consider your safety...."

She turned and bumped open the door with her derriere. "Voilà."

"Damn it, Lacey."

Her lush lips puckered into a provocative smile. She reached for his hand. Pulling him inside, she kissed him again, the curve of her smile caressing the hollow of his cheek. "Darlin', you're man enough to keep me safe."

Somewhere along the way she'd discarded the sweat jacket, and her breasts were round and soft against his chest. One of her thighs rubbed between his. *Oh, man, oh, man,* he thought. She was working it. She was coming on like a runaway train. Pure seduction.

"I'll bet you can keep me safe all night long," she purred.

He didn't want to be seduced. He wanted to take a wild, spontaneous tumble into ecstasy with the Goddess of Hot Fudge Sundaes.

"Mmm, Alec," she coaxed, pressing against the hard, straining part of him that only *wanted.*

He was weak. He kissed her again, hard and fierce, searching for the woman beneath the black velvet.

She was there. Wide eyes, racy curves; sweetly feminine, openly lusty. And so vulnerable it overwhelmed him that she had bared her emotions and placed her trust in him. After so many months of stark self-reliance, it was too much for him to handle. And yet too much for him to refuse.

"We'll have a serious talk tomorrow," she promised, the lilt in her voice saying the opposite as she took both of his hands in hers and led him to the love seat.

The ache of containing his hunger for her was acute.

He told himself that sex didn't have to be a manipulation or a complication. It could just be sex. Clearly Lacey wasn't worrying over words like *commitment* and *relationship* and…

Love.

Now *that* would be a complication. Good thing it didn't apply.

There was no love in the fathomless blue depths of Lacey's eyes, or the beckoning sweep of her lashes, or the pout of her ripe lips—only seduction. None in the deep, glowering heat he felt inside when he fit his hand around her breast and his thumb rubbed hard against the bud of her nipple through her cotton print dress— that was only carnal desire. Her low moan, the scrape of her red nails on his jaw, the fingers she buried in the long hair at his nape as he drew his tongue along her collarbone…none of that was love. It was two adults, man and woman, reduced to elemental physical need.

Not love.

Lacey's back arched as he scooped her breasts together, pressing them up into the low round neckline of her dress. Her fingers tightened in the roots of his hair, and the small sharp pain became part of his aching hunger. "I want you," she said, tormenting him further by rocking her hips against his uncomfortable erection. It was an excruciating torture. "Please."

He found her mouth again, her warm, sweet mouth, and lost the last of his restraint in their kiss. "Right here?" he asked, his lips plucking at hers, nibbling, sucking, biting.

She sighed appreciatively. "The bedroom."

"Yes." No worry about serious conversations now; they seemed to be capable only of monosyllables.

"We should—" Her eyes went round as he slid one hand under her dress, over the woolen tights and her taut belly, all the way up to her breasts. He shoved her bra out of the way and roughly stroked her nipples by rubbing his callused palm back and forth, back and forth. "Bed," she gasped, closing her eyes tight.

"Right." Measuring her response by the tiny quivering spasms of each eyelid, he continued to chafe her breasts, rolling the nipples on each stroke. She curled the tip of her tongue against her upper lip, humming with pleasure.

"Alec," she pleaded, her hips beginning to writhe in sync with the erotic sway of her breasts. "Bed." She sank lower into the cushions. *"Now."*

He didn't know what came over him. Maybe it was Lacey's influence or her melting reaction to his rough caress; maybe it was his own need to conquer, to claim. But he stood and put his shoulder to her midsection and hoisted her up off the love seat in one motion so strong and fluid that her not inconsiderable weight wound up slung across his shoulder like a sack of oats. "Alec!" she said, gulping back an astonished laugh. She braced herself and tried to wiggle free but he had one arm coiled tight around her hips and the other clamped to the back of her thighs.

"Who are you calling he-man?" he challenged, tromping toward the half-open bedroom door.

Lacey's hair swung in a glossy waterfall down his back. "Only you," she said with a smile in her voice. "Forever after, only you."

He kicked open the door to the dark bedroom and stood stock-still in his tracks. Or someone else's, he realized, his instincts on fire—*but too late,* too late—his desire slowly deflating, punctured by dread.

Lacey squirmed. "Alec, nice as the view is—" she patted his rear end "—I'd like to get down now, okay?"

He dumped her off his shoulder. "The front door was locked, wasn't it?" She turned, her face drawn into a mask, all fun and games forgotten. "I think I'm going to have a talk with that doorman of yours," Alec said flatly, and flicked on the light switch.

The first thing Lacey saw was one of her black velvet dresses laid out very neatly in the exact center of the bed. Strewn across it were several roses crudely stripped of their blossoms. The thorn-tipped stem of one of them had been threaded through a pair of silver handcuffs. She closed her eyes and opened them again, telling herself this wasn't happening, but the crushed scarlet petals sprinkled over her Battenburg lace pillow shams still looked like droplets of congealed blood.

When her knees buckled, Alec put his arm around her, holding her up in what seemed a gruesome parody of their frantic passion in the elevator. "Damn him," Lacey said of Mr. X, filled with anger that an invasion of such ugliness should have ruined what was perfect and private between her and Alec.

Then she saw the knife.

And then she got afraid.

"POOR COUNTESS PUSHKIN," Lacey said miserably, preferring to focus on the deep knife slashes through the dummy's wicker torso rather than the emotional damage done to herself by the break-in. "To come to such an end."

Alec wrapped her hands around a plastic cup of hot coffee. The kitchen was being preserved for fingerprints, so the takeout cappuccino had been provided by the worried, apologetic doorman, who'd also wordlessly retrieved the wig and glasses and duffel they'd dropped in the elevator. "Go on, drink up," Alec said.

"You can use the caffeine. We've got a long night ahead of us."

"You called the police?" She thought that he might have, but she'd been too shocked to pay close attention.

"They'll take a while to get here. We'll both have to wait. I don't want to send you to the hotel alone." After the police, he explained, he'd called the hotel he'd checked out of only that morning to reserve a double room for what was left of the night.

Lacey shuddered, unable to concentrate on mundane details when all she could think of was how a butcher knife from her own kitchen had been plunged into the countess's slashed bosom, pinning a piece of Lacey's own embossed stationery in place. The word *vixen* had been scrawled across the page in lipstick—her own red lipstick.

Mr. X's threats had gotten extremely personal.

Nonetheless, she tried to put on a show of bravado. "It was a shock at first, but it was also pretty amateur, don't you think? Mr. X is not an original thinker. I mean, come on—stripped roses, cheap handcuffs, a note written in lipstick and stuck in place with a knife? Sounds like a TV movie. Woman-in-jeopardy." She laughed hollowly. "Maybe someone from Hollywood will buy the rights. I can play myself playing Madame X."

"Drink your coffee," Alec said. He didn't want to encourage her high-pitched diatribe, but she was right about the incident being more theatrical than harmful. If it wasn't for the fact that there was no visible sign of a break-in, he wouldn't have to be as worried as he was. An amateur with an obsession was one thing; an amateur with an obsession and easy access was another.

He had to find out from Lacey who might have keys to the apartment, but didn't want to start on the subject while they were still occupying said apartment. She was frightened enough, despite her stubborn refusal to give in to it.

As he paced the living room, Alec watched her sip at the coffee, her expression shifting from anger to worry to plucky determination. She was a fighter; that was good, though if he did his job correctly it wouldn't come down to that. *If* he did his job…

Alec cursed under his breath. He hadn't been doing his job tonight. He'd been getting his rocks off.

And Lacey was too generous to see that his lapse of control, his sheer carelessness, had put her life in danger.

"Come sit down, Alec," she said, moving her shoulders restively against the cushions of the love seat. "You're making me nervous, pacing that way."

He sat, but only because he had to talk plain and maybe tough to her. This time she had to listen. "Lacey. I know you don't care to follow orders, but tomorrow I'm getting you out of this city. If you want to complain, go tell it to Countess Pushkin. And if you even think of refusing—well, I've already proven I can put you over my shoulder."

"Really! I'm…" She stopped herself, forehead puckering, then tried again in a milder voice. "Okay, Alec, you win. I'm agreeable to making a short-term escape."

"You are?" He hadn't expected her to give in so quickly.

"I can't stay here anyway," she said, glancing regretfully around the still partly unpacked apartment. "It's not the roses and the knife that bother me as much as the thought of *him*—prowling around the rooms, paw-ing through my belongings." She grimaced. "*Touching* things." She put the coffee down and hugged herself with crisscrossed arms. "I don't think I'll ever be comfortable here again...."

Alec wanted to gather her up and hold her close and comfort her, but he didn't do it. He was her bodyguard. *He was her bodyguard.*

Lacey folded her knees up to her chin and hugged them, too. "So, where do we go?"

"I know a place."

Her eyes rolled. "More secretive spy games, huh, Al—" She stopped, stricken by the implication of what she'd intended as a joke. "Wait. I didn't mean to, um, imply..."

So she knew. Alec's mind went blank as a TV screen for a moment, then clicked back on at a higher volume. Lacey knew about his past. She knew that he'd been accused, disgraced, dismissed. And still she'd wanted to sleep with him....

There was no accounting for taste.

"Forget it," he said, to forestall the stammering apologies—and perhaps questions—that would come next. "Do you want Jericho to find you another bodyguard? I have contacts. I can call—"

"What? Of course not!" She reached for his hands, her eyes bright and begging for contact. For reconnection.

Alec couldn't give it to her. Not now.

He stood and walked away.

LACEY AND ALEC RETURNED to the apartment the next day, as stiff and silent with each other as Buckingham Palace guards. For once Lacey wasn't playing the cavorting tourist desperate for a laugh. She wasn't in the mood. It had been early morning by the time the police had finished questioning her about the break-in. Afterward, she'd stood aside while Alec checked them into the hotel, blearily grateful that he was there to handle the details.

There'd been no underlying sexual tension about sharing a room. She'd barely glanced at Alec, just kicked off her boots, skinned out of the tights, wrapped herself in a blanket and fallen into bed, exhausted. One good thing about not wearing makeup was that you didn't have to wash it off, she thought, grateful for that, too, as she burrowed into a deep, dreamless sleep.

Alec woke her at seven-thirty a.m. His bed didn't appear to have been slept in, but he looked fresh and alert and primed for action in tailored trousers and a nubby black crewneck sweater with a half-inch of crisp white collar showing at his throat. Comb lines cut through his damp hair where it had been swept straight back off his face.

Of course, Lacey thought grumpily, he'd had his own razor and fresh clothing to work with, whereas she had only the same old duffel bag. Forced to discard her usual elaborate beauty ritual, she groped her way to the bathroom for a long, hot, soapy shower. Her wardrobe situation amounted to a poor choice between inappropriate velvet and wrinkled cotton, so she steeled herself and put on yesterday's underwear and the anti–Madame X dress, then tightly braided her wet hair. That would have to do for Alec. She wasn't going to wear the wig.

Their breakfast had arrived by the time she came out of the bathroom. Alec issued a few terse edicts while she nibbled toast and stared distastefully at the spongy flesh of an overripe cantaloupe. Imagine that. Mr. X had stolen her appetite.

Or maybe it was Alec's fault for turning her world

upside down—in his own way. She studied him silently. He was still going on about credit cards and telephone calls, and while she might have stopped him by bringing up what had almost happened between them, as well as her inadvertent stumble into his verboten past, she knew the timing wasn't right. Alec was in his lockstep, no-back-talk mode.

After more instructions, more arrangements and a quick call to Jericho, Alec escorted Lacey back to her apartment to, as he put it, "pick up a few essentials." She, however, intended to pack all of her cosmetics and a good portion of her wardrobe—there was no telling when she'd get out from under Alec's thumb, and a woman had to be prepared for anything, fashionwise—until she was actually faced with doing so. The gritty fingerprint powder that the police had left on nearly every surface was disheartening. Worse was the trespasser's lingering aura. Lacey felt as though anything he might have touched—which was *every*thing—carried an invisible but indelible stain.

She tried to cheer herself with the thought that it was an excuse to buy a whole new wardrobe.

The doorman buzzed, but she didn't stop her desultory packing to answer the summons. Alec would insist on handling it, anyway.

Right on cue, he called, "Lacey?"

She saluted and threw a few more things into her suitcase, mumbling, "Right away, sir."

"Lacey!"

She snapped shut her suitcase and raised her voice to a sweetness as artificial as aspartame. "Coming, darlin'." One last glance around the bedroom. The roses, handcuffs, velvet dress and slashed dressmaker's dummy had been photographed and then removed as evidence, so the room appeared normal enough. Just the same, she knew she'd rather not come back.

Alec was standing by the door, his expression dark as storm clouds. "Did you call Piper Hicks from the hotel?"

Lacey set down her suitcase. "Yes, I did."

"I told you to call no one."

"Well, now, I couldn't leave town without explanation, could I? Piper will have to cancel my upcoming appearances, so I left a message about the break-in with her secretary."

"You weren't supposed to—"

"Yes, yes, I know," she interrupted impatiently. "But Piper is my agent, Alec. She's not Mr. X."

"Perhaps, but how do you know he's not someone from her office? You've come into contact with Piper's employees, I imagine. And many of them have access to your personal information."

Lacey's mouth snapped shut. "I hadn't considered that angle," she conceded tightly. "Even so, I don't see what reason any of them would have to—"

"You're still making the mistake of believing that Mr. X is a rational person." Alec cocked his head, listening for the rattling sound of the rising elevator. "Piper Hicks is on her way up. Before she gets here, let me reiterate." He ticked off points one by one. "Until this situation is resolved, you are not to telephone anyone, including friends, family or business associates. Don't write, don't send postcards. No checkbooks, no ATM withdrawals. No credit cards—"

"How am I supposed to pay my way?" she asked, outraged. There went the new wardrobe.

"Where we're going, you won't have to." The doorbell rang. Alec checked the peephole, said, "Tell your agent as little as possible," and opened the door.

"That elevator is a death trap," Piper Hicks pro-
nounced. She removed her sunglasses and stepped
warily into the small foyer, her sharp eyes shooting
from Alec's face to Lacey's to the unconventional living room beyond. The thin brown lines of her brows
arched even higher up her forehead. "Lacey, dear."
She craned her neck to kiss the air near her client's pale
cheek. "Even though you look like a bag lady, I'm glad
to see that you're in one piece. Now, what is this nonsense about leaving the city?"

"I don't really want to—"

"Then you shan't," Piper said firmly. "I'm certain
you haven't forgotten the reading we scheduled in that
rather cramped but prestigious Soho bookstore? I'm
told Madame X has quite a following among a certain
flamboyant element of the intelligentsia."

"Cancel it," Alec said, just as firmly.

Piper's hands fluttered, making her diamond rings
flash ostentatiously. "As my client, Lacey, I think you
know your responsibilities." She trained her eyes on
the other woman's perplexed face. "We don't allow
minor annoyances to disrupt us, do we, dear? We're
troopers, one and all. The show must go on, et cetera, et
cetera."

Lacey shook her head—reluctantly. "I'm sorry,
Piper. I can't stay."

The agent drew herself up. "Well, then."

"The police were here," Lacey said desperately. "I'm
sure they'll find out who's behind this very, very soon,
and then I can come back. Maybe you could just re-
schedule the reading? And whatever else is coming up
for, say, the next week or two?"

"*All That Glitters* is shot on a very tight schedule."
Piper's voice was brittle with disapproval. "They will

not hold up production to accommodate the foibles of a prima donna."

Alec's eyes blazed. "Lacey is not playing the prima donna, Mrs. Hicks. She's in very real danger. You might be concerned for her safety rather than her career."

"Really." Piper barely glanced at him. "Dear child," she said to Lacey, oozing concern, "of course we at Piper Hicks, Inc. will take care of everything. We'll hire the very best security firm in the business to look after you. There's no need to worry on that account."

"Oh," Lacey said. "That's very...thoughtful."

"If a bit tardy," Alec murmured.

Piper smiled determinedly. "Are we all settled, then, dear?" She eyed the unpacked boxes and papier-mâché trees in the living room. "Perhaps my people should make a reservation at the Plaza for you while they're at it? My treat, of course, until the security detail is in place."

"Well, gosh, I..." Nervously Lacey tried to smooth the wrinkles from her baggy print dress. "I don't know what to say." She hesitated, then looked up. "Alec...?"

Though his demeanor was stoic, she could see the slight tick of muscles tensing in his jaw. And the fierce gleam of his cut-glass eyes. "It seems you have a decision to make," he said, his voice as tense as it was soft.

Piper's polite laugh sounded like a trickling brook. "Not really a difficult choice, is it?"

Lacey stepped back, weighing her options. Surprisingly, Piper was right; the choice wasn't difficult.

She could pick Piper Hicks, Inc., the Plaza, a flank of Armani-suited bodyguards, impending fame and fortune.

Or Alec and a trip to a mystery destination—without credit cards.

Easy enough, she told herself, *if you follow the instincts of your heart.*

She tipped up her chin, emotion welling within her, and said, "I'm going with Alec."

7

"You little vixen."

He'd followed Laryssa up to her suite, uncertain but aroused. He turned to place her parcels on a Biedermeier console by the door; she went to warm herself by the fire one of the efficient maids must have lit on their arrival. When he looked back, Laryssa was slowly removing her clothing piece by piece.

She shed the hat and fitted velvet jacket. The black-and-gray striped skirt rustled as it dropped. An ivory blouse drifted to the carpet. Smiling bewitchingly, she hunched her shoulders so her lace bra slid down her arms to reveal a pretty pair of creamy, speckled breasts. Turning, she stepped delicately out of her underpants, kicked the mound of clothing aside and posed for him like an erotic Victorian painting, firelight licking her pale skin and the rippling russet hair spread across her shoulders. She wore nothing but opaque black, thigh-high stockings and her tightly laced boots, with her hands still tucked into the strategically positioned black velvet muff.

"You little vixen," he said, his eyes blazing. "You cunning little vixen."

And then he went for her.

ALEC TOOK THE TURNPIKE south out of New York, and by the time they'd bypassed Philadelphia, Lacey was pretty sure she knew where they were going. For the first hour of the drive she'd occupied herself by fretting over her on-hold career and how to mend the cracks in her relationship with Piper, but underneath she felt quite certain of her choice. Which, considering her long struggle for success and her previously tenacious hold on what she'd gained, made no sense at all.

Or more sense than she cared to admit, she thought, a pleasurable warmth rising inside her when she glanced at Alec. One glance was all it took to remind her of how much she already wanted him, and needed him, and...*liked* him. Even though he was presently treating her like a chore.

A *chore*, she scoffed, comforting herself with the memory of the way he'd looked when she'd said she'd go with him. It hadn't been a put-out-the-trash-and-set-the-table expression.

Alec flicked on the radio. Ten minutes of classical music on National Public Radio had Lacey scrambling for her duffel bag, positive she'd thrown a few CDs in among her other junk. "How about some Sarah McLachlan or Tracy Chapman," she suggested. "Ani DeFranco?"

"Lilith Fair fare?" Alec was dubious. "Not for me, thanks."

"Lilith Fair was fabulous. I loved Lilith Fair. I went twice."

"There isn't a CD player in the truck," he said, not regretfully.

She was nonplussed by this lack of what she considered a vital convenience, on a par with air-conditioning and cruise control. "Well, that's just dumb, Alec."

"I prefer to call it simple."

She grinned. "Simpleminded."

"Uncluttered. Streamlined. After I left..." Alec hesitated, and for a moment Lacey thought he was going to reveal something significant about his past. Instead, his grip on the steering wheel tightened. "Well, let's just say that I recognize the benefits of an uncomplicated life."

"Hmm." Lacey mulled that over, but she knew it was useless to try to get anything else out of him. He would tell her about the Zhabekistan scandal when he was ready. When he trusted her.

They stopped for lunch at a fast-food place outside of Baltimore. Afterward, Lacey put her long legs to use and beat Alec to the driver's side. "I want to drive."

"You don't know where we're going."

She turned her level stare on him. "To your place, of course. To your farm in Virginia." With a self-satisfied wiggle, she scooted behind the wheel. "You can give me directions—" her thumb jerked to the right "—from the shotgun seat."

The corners of his eyes crinkled when he smiled. She found that charming. "Can you drive a stick shift?" he asked.

With a whoop she turned the key and revved the engine. "Darlin', I learned on a stick. Grandma Lacey-Beth drove a '66 Chevy with a rusted-out muffler and a cracked windshield."

Once they were back on the road, Lacey added as an afterthought, purely to bedevil him, "'Course, it's true that I also once left the truck in neutral and it rolled into the swimming hole...."

She crowed at his look of consternation, but then he surprised her by wisecracking, "Talk about flooding the engine," and she moaned at the feeble joke.

They talked for a while about cars, then the hassle of

keeping one in Manhattan, and then how both of them thought that taking a road trip across the entire country would be cool. Lacey was deep into describing her *Thelma and Louise* fantasy before she noticed that Alec had slumped against the door and dozed off. She smiled fondly at him, remembering that he probably hadn't slept in a day and a half.

"You had a little catnap," she murmured, when he came awake again only a few minutes later.

He raked his hands through his hair, looked thoughtfully at her and said, "Yeah," in a hushed voice. Lacey wondered confusedly if he'd revealed something significant, after all.

By the time they'd crossed the state line into Virginia, there had been only one minor instance of gear grinding and some raucous catcalls from a car full of college guys who'd either recognized Lacey or just wanted to express their appreciation of the figure she cut at the wheel of the pickup. While Alec tried to glare them down, Lacey simply waved cheerfully and swerved the truck across two lanes of traffic, leaving the college students stuck behind a soccer mom in a behemoth of a van.

Alec gave Lacey directions to Webster Station, the small, quaint town nearest to his farm. The brush with the college guys had reminded them both of Lacey's celebrity, and that they were fugitives from it. When they stopped at a grocery store for provisions, Alec made her put a scarf over her hair and wait in the pickup while he went inside alone. She complied, grumpy at the thought of her upcoming isolation. Then she reconsidered, and became light-headed and dizzy and tingly all over at the thought of her upcoming isolation...with Alec.

Her heart lurched. Had she risked her career and her

contract with a high-powered agent merely for a week alone with Alec? Was she that crazy?

Crazy in love?

"What's the matter?" Alec asked, heaving two paper sacks of groceries into the bed of the pickup.

"Nothing," she insisted.

"I'm driving," he said, not believing her. "You don't look good." He watched warily as she clambered over the gearshift, her legs crossing like a blue-jeaned pretzel. "Try not to be sick in the truck. We're almost home."

"I'm not sick," she said thickly. "But thanks for your concern."

"It must be the chili dog and double order of cheese fries you ate at lunch."

She looked out the window so she wouldn't have to look at him, worrying about his upholstery—hah! "You snitched half the fries, and, anyway, I have a cast-iron stomach." *But a heart like a marshmallow.*

He shrugged and told her his place was nine miles outside of town. Rockridge Road climbed gradually into the foothills of the Blue Ridge Mountains, through some of the prettiest countryside Lacey had ever seen once she stopped thinking of being in love with Alec and started looking out of the window for real. The leaves had turned—orange, gold and vermilion—and were so bright and sharp edged in the setting sun that she had to narrow her eyes.

"Here." Alec took the anti–Madame X sunglasses off the dash and handed them to her.

Her stomach did a slow, sensuous roll. "Thanks," she said, shoving the glasses in place and quickly turning back to the window. *Oh, Lacey, Lacey, get ahold of yourself,* she ordered, jolted by the emotion that had swept through her just because Alec was observant and thoughtful and kind and brave.

Trying to stay calm, she stared at the green hills, dazzling trees and Technicolor sunset. So what? she asked herself. So what if he gave her coffee when she was scared, laughed at her dopey farmer's walk, was willing to risk being blown up by a letter bomb—even though it had been only a thong, it *could* have been a bomb—and kissed a zillion times better than Lars Torberg, heartthrob of the silver screen?

So what, you say? Lacey almost laughed out loud at herself. The better question was so what else did she want? And while the easy answer might be that she wanted nothing else, Alec was enough, that wasn't strictly true. She wanted fame and fortune and fancy dress, too. Even after everything that had happened, she still wanted it all.

Whereas Alec had already had more than enough.

THE DISPLAY OF expensive horseflesh, rolling green pastures and white board fencing looked like Kentucky to Lacey, but what did she know? Alec's ramrod posture managed to straighten by one more prideful degree as the pickup crunched over the curved gravel road and the house and barn came into view. The house was a white, two-story colonial with dark green shutters, the barn—or stable—similarly styled in red brick and white siding. Two cupolas crowned the gray slate roof. Lacey shaded her eyes from the sun to make out the verdigris copper weather vanes spinning against the darkening indigo sky.

"Wow," she said, sliding from the truck. Everything in sight looked either newly mowed or freshly scrubbed and painted. It was a far cry from the catch-as-catch-can style of her various shabby apartments.

"Bodyguarding and horse breeding must pay very well." She put her hand over her mouth. "Whoops. 'Scuse me. That was a crass comment."

Alec wasn't concerned. "It's taken me a year of steady work to bring this place up to standard. But you haven't seen the inside of the house yet—I've only started there."

A gleaming sorrel filly craned her neck over the paddock fence and whickered to Alec. "The horses look extremely well cared for," Lacey said, although she had no comparison other than her grandma's scruffy old mare. "How many do you have?"

"Only a dozen or so at the moment. This is a small operation, and I sent most of the yearlings to the fall auction." He walked to the fence and slid his hand under the feathers of the young horse's flaxen mane. "There you go, baby," he crooned, rubbing her crest. "So itchy, aren't you?"

Telling herself she wasn't jealous of a horse, for goodness' sake, Lacey tucked her hands into the cuffs of her fisherman's sweater and ambled over to join Alec and his adoration society. The filly stretched out her neck in bliss, her top lip curling up to show a set of impressive choppers. "I think she's in love," Lacey said, staying out of chomping distance. "What's her name?"

"Trillium." Alec slapped the filly's satiny shoulder. "I bought several broodmares at auction last summer, with foals at their side. Trillium's the best of the young ones. I'm going to keep her."

Lacey nudged her toe against the rickrack brick border between grass and gravel, recalling what little he'd told her about his early life. "How did you ever manage to learn about horses when you were following your father from embassy to embassy as a kid? Or is this a recent interest?"

"No, I went to a school in England for several years, where equestrian skills were part of the curriculum. But you can find horse lovers everywhere. In Egypt, I worked with purebred Arabians at the royal stables. Later, I studied the German theories of jumping and dressage. And the vaqueros of South America are amazing.…"

Lacey watched Trillium walk away, head down, nostrils whiffling the grass. "Sounds like you've lived everywhere, Alec."

"Except small town, U.S.A.," he said. "Living here is a new experience for me."

She leaned against the board fence, eyes sweeping from the barn and various outbuildings back to the house. It was quite a spread, but not so large or ritzy to be intimidating. The rays of the setting sun glinted on the front door's brass carriage lamps; blue shadows crept across the velvety lawn. She sighed, with pleasure as much as regret. "It's beautiful here, Alec."

"But…?"

She flipped her braid over her shoulder. Might as well lay it on the line. "But I'm a big-city girl. You knew that going in."

Alec hooked his boot on the bottom rail and squinted toward the stable paddock, where Trillium and several of the other horses were waiting for their dinner. His voice came out rusty. "It won't hurt you to get some fresh air in your lungs for a week or two." He cleared his throat, and when the horses nickered restlessly he tossed Lacey his keys without quite looking at her. "Can you let yourself into the house? I've got work to do in the stable."

She snatched the keys from the air, taken aback by his abrupt dismissal. "Sure, I guess."

The jostling horses nipped and squealed at each other as Alec approached. "Don't forget the groceries," he called, without turning.

Lacey saluted the back of his head.

ALEC COULD HAVE KICKED himself. He scooped and measured oats, telling himself what a lunkhead he was. Here was this woman—this warm, generous, lively, sexy woman—offering to be his friend, and maybe more—*definitely* more—and he was restraining himself, letting his past come between them. Had his monkish self-punishment become habit, or was he simply as dumb as a post?

Both, he thought with disgust, dusting off his hands as he walked out of the feed room. But he could still change that.

Peter Bellingham, the redheaded college student who worked part-time at the farm, walked into the stable with Dodger dancing at his heels. Dodger stopped and stared, whining in her throat, until Alec slapped his leg and said, "C'mere, girl." Then the dog flew like a fuzzy brown rocket down the row of stalls and threw herself against his legs. He knelt and she whimpered and licked his face, squirming and quivering and jumping in his arms.

He wasn't such a bad guy, Alec decided, if Dodger liked him so much. A week after he'd moved into the large, bleak, empty house, he'd gone to the pound, and Dodger had picked him to be her owner, which meant that he had to have some redeeming qualities. Dodger was very discriminating.

"Hey, boss, you're back from the big city," said Pete. "For good?"

"That depends." Alec straightened, deciding to take Dodger over to the house and see what happened when she met Lacey. "Take care of the horses tonight, will you, Pete? There's something I have to do."

JUGGLING HER SUITCASE, the duffel and one bag of groceries, Lacey let herself into Alec's house. The black-and-white diamond-patterned foyer was dim with shadows, empty except for a *demi-lune* table against the wall and a once-elegant wooden staircase that was missing half its spindles. She dumped her luggage at the bottom step and went to find the kitchen.

The living room was clean, warm, cozily paneled—very masculine. It was furnished with a rolltop desk and a massive, cushy, slipcovered couch and armchair placed before the brick fireplace. Two worn Persian rugs ran diagonally across pegged, honey-colored floorboards. Lacey switched on a stained-glass lamp and went into the next room.

The dining room wasn't as welcoming. The only furnishings were an oval table with Windsor chairs and a sideboard that needed refinishing. Water-stained wallpaper was peeling off the walls; the limp curtains at the windows looked like they'd hung there forever. The kitchen was a relief, though. It was large and square, with a brick floor, oak trim and banks of wooden cabinets painted white.

While Lacey was opening various cabinets, familiarizing herself with their contents, Alec came in the back door with the other sack of groceries. He stood for a moment, just looking at her; she shivered as though he'd run a cold fingertip along her bare back. "I'm sorry," he finally said, going over to put ice cream in the freezer. "That was rude of me, taking off on you like that."

She stowed a box of granola in its proper place before speaking. "It's okay, Alec. I can fend for myself. It's not like you're running a bed-and-breakfast."

A curly, brown, medium-size mutt trotted into view. It stopped and peered at Lacey through a frazzled forelock, its damp brown nose quivering suspiciously. "Lacey, this is Dodger," Alec said. "Dodger, Lacey. Be nice, will you, girl?"

"Who, me?" Lacey asked, blinking at Dodger, who blinked back at her. The dog sniffed the air, shook herself, then walked over to Alec and nudged his leg, hind end deliberately pointed at Lacey. Another member of Alec's adoration society, she decided, wondering how many more would pop out of the woodwork. There was probably a bright, bouncy farmer's daughter who brought him casseroles and sympathy. And a flashy young divorcée who brought takeout Chinese and her diaphragm. Fortunately, Alec didn't seem the type to take up either offer.

Not the sympathy, at any rate.

"You don't like dogs?" he asked, sounding disappointed.

"Umm…" She stalled. Was this a test? "I wanted a puppy when I was a kid, but my mom said my dad was allergic. I think she just didn't want dog hair on the upholstery." Lacey put away a box of no-salt crackers. "Grandma Stuart had canaries, and Grandma Lacey-Beth had five cats. For the mice."

"Oh," Alec said, watching Dodger studiously ignore Lacey.

"Is this a problem, me not being a dog person? So long as Dodger doesn't bite me or steal my steak, I'll leave her alone."

Alec sighed. "Maybe that's best."

If it had been a test, she'd flunked. Lacey opened another cupboard, looking for dog munchies. If it mattered so much to Alec, she'd make friends with the mutt. No problem. She could make friends with anyone.

She ripped open a package of cookies, bit into one and extended the other half to Dodger. "Here, girl." She leaned over and waggled the cookie. "Poochie, poochie, here's a cookie."

Dodger's perpetually wagging tail went still; she wouldn't even deign to turn her head. Lacey aimed her Marilyn smile at Alec—he looked seriously concerned—and popped the cookie in her mouth. "Don't worry," she said, crunching, "we'll make friends, I promise."

He shrugged. "Let me show you the bedrooms."

Lacey took another cookie before she followed him, whispering, "None for you, then, Dodger," even though the dog was still pretending she didn't exist. If cookies didn't work, bacon would. She'd get up early and pop some in the microwave on the sly, and Alec would be so impressed with Dodger's change of heart that he'd—

Lacey stopped herself, so aghast she almost inhaled the last bite of the cookie. She must be nuts. *Getting up early?* She liked to sleep late. *Nuking bacon?* She tried to never make a mess in any kitchen she might have to clean. *Bribing a mutt, a dumb mutt, to impress a man?* She would never sink so low!

"Here you go." Alec set down her luggage. "This will be your room."

She coughed up cookie crumbs. "Nice," she said, running her tongue around her teeth. The bedroom was spare but sophisticated, with clean white walls, oak trim and nubby linen scarves draped at the windows. The Noguchi lamp and stark black lacquer bed were minimalist in design, but the plump pillows and thick tan-and-ivory-checked comforter were chosen strictly for comfort.

Lacey had an insight. "But this is your room!"

Alec tried to demur. "It's the best bedroom. I want you to have it."

She picked up the parachute duffel and said, "No, I'll sleep in one of the other rooms," when what she really wanted to say was that they could share, couldn't they? Wouldn't that be cozy? Wouldn't that be fine?

Alec kept insisting until Lacey had another insight. "Dodger sleeps here, too, doesn't she? If I displace Dodger, we'll never be friends."

Fortunately, he saw the logic in that, and they switched rooms, with Lacey assuring him that the only other inhabitable bedroom, with its tarnished brass bed and no nightstand, was just super—she *liked* cracked, stained, crumbling plaster, she really did, in fact she knew a trompe l'oeil artist who reproduced the look in Park Avenue co-ops for big bucks.

Finally Alec left to start dinner and Lacey unpacked, trying to decide if she should dress for dinner or *un*-dress for dinner. Would Alec like her as an appetizer? Would he like her served up beside the mashed potatoes? Would she make a good dessert? Would she ever stop thinking about making love with Alec and actually get to do it?

She closed her eyes, fell facedown on the blue-and-white quilt and lay there spread-eagled for ten mind-bending minutes, then got up, washed her face, fixed her hair and went downstairs so she could stare dopily at Alec while he made dinner.

Her and Dodger.

LACEY YAWNED and said, "This is really nice, really cozy."

Alec looked up from his book. After dinner, they'd washed dishes, checked on the horses, then come back inside to build a fire. Lacey had seemed content to sit quietly and stare into the flames while he read. She was curled into the armchair in her sweater and jeans, her socks drooping at the toes, her eyes heavy-lidded. Her hair was spread across her shoulders and the back of the chair, a wild, kinky mass burnished by the firelight.

She was probably bored to tears. "Not what you're used to, I imagine," he said. "But there's no nightlife to speak of in Webster Station—unless you count country line dancing at the Loblolly Club."

She suppressed a smile. "When can we go?"

"We can't. Someone might recognize you."

"And report back to Mr. X? Sounds pretty far-fetched."

"You never know." What he did know was that he wanted to keep her close, all to himself, and that was not what he'd intended when he'd accepted this assignment. What had happened to the emotional distance that was supposed to guarantee his detachment?

Lacey threw one leg over the arm of the overstuffed chair. "What are you reading?"

"Uh…" He looked at the cover of the book as if he was surprised to find it in his hand. Knowing he should lie and say something dull like *Bleak House*, he said, "'Black Velvet Vixen,'" which was the truth. The dangerous truth.

Lacey's eyes widened. "Aha—so you couldn't resist. You went out and bought yourself a copy of the book."

"Actually, it so happens I liberated it from a box of books in your apartment. I hope you don't mind."

She put her arms over her head and stretched, her

bulky sweater riding up to reveal a narrow strip of creamy skin above the waistband of her jeans. Nothing spectacular, but the sight of it made him want to get down on his knees before her and grovel for a kiss, a taste…a lick. "Want to read out loud to me?" she asked, her lips curling into another of her teasing smiles.

"That wouldn't be a good idea." Alec shifted, making Dodger, who'd been stretched along the length of the couch beside him, groan and roll until she was draped over his feet like a curly brown foot warmer. He held up the book, a finger marking his page. "This is strictly research."

"I'll bet. And you read *Playboy* for the articles, too."

Lacey was a centerfold if he'd ever seen one. A living, breathing centerfold, but also so much more. And that was what was so damn hard to resist.

She stretched again, her breasts shifting under the sweater, her hips arching off the cushion before she wiggled them back into place.

Well, that and the rest of her, he admitted.

"Catch." She threw him a big, squashy pillow. "You're going to need that, if you keep on reading." At his mystified expression, she lifted her eyebrows and said knowingly, "For your…lap."

Heat swept through him like an arid desert wind. "I can control myself," he said, but he kept the pillow.

And she noticed.

He tried to get back to Amalie's story, but kept reading the same line over and over: "Wild, untamed creatures born of fire and desire and ravening need…"

When he looked up, Lacey was watching him, her face pink from the warmth of the fire. "Finding any clues about Mr. X?"

Alec closed the book. *Concentrate*, he told himself,

and thought of Lacey's smooth skin. Her laugh. Her legs—oh, man, her long legs. *Concentrate on something else.*

"Vixen," he said huskily. "That's Mr. X's running theme. Lying vixen, conniving vixen, two-faced vixen—"

"Lovely," she murmured.

"What does it bring to mind?"

She punched one fist into the soft, rumpled cushions of the chair. "I don't know! I don't want to even think about it."

"You have to. We both do. How much time can the police devote to a nonviolent crime? They've already eliminated Malcolm—his handwriting sample didn't match the letters—so they're at a dead end. Even though I'm a bodyguard, not a detective, it occurs to me that if you want to get back to your life as Madame X—" *please stay here forever* "—then we're going to have to figure this out ourselves. So think. Vixen," he coaxed her. "Vixen. Free-associate if you have to."

"All right." She sighed and leaned her head against the chair, eyes half-closed. "Vixen. Shrew. *Taming of the Shrew.*" She looked at him, brightening. "Hey. Bet you'd never guess that I starred in *Taming of the Shrew* in high school."

"Some stretch."

She laughed. "Yeah, I know."

"Back to vixen, though…"

Ignoring him, she threw her arms wide and began to emote. "'Your betters have endured me say my mind,/ And if you cannot, best you stop your ears./My tongue will tell…'" Her voice trailed off. Alec thought it was because she'd forgotten the rest of the quote, but then he looked up and saw the deep sapphire glint of her welling eyes. "Alec," she murmured.

He didn't respond.

She took a deep breath and leaned forward, her rich voice shaking with emotion. "'My tongue will tell the anger of my heart,/Or else my heart, concealing it, will break.'"

Alec swallowed the lump in his throat. He looked away, toward the leaping flames. "'The anger of my heart,'" he said softly and Lacey started to come up out of her chair. He put his palm up to stop her.

She sank back again, her hands clasping and unclasping between her knees. "Please. I didn't intend to push you—"

"Let me think."

"Don't think, Alec. *Feel.*"

A charred log fell, sending a plume of glittering sparks up the chimney. At the same moment anger and sorrow flared hotly in Alec, scorching his heart...but melting his resistance. "You are a vixen," he said to Lacey, loving the gentle curve of her cheek, the curl of her lashes, the concern that showed so clearly on her face. "A cunning little vixen."

Her head wagged slowly from side to side. "No. I only want—"

"I know. And I think I finally realize that I want, too. I want to forget my past, I want a fresh start. And I want you." He stood and walked over to her, smoothing his hands over her cheeks, soothing her worry, tilting her face so it made a perfect firelit oval against the extravagance of her cascading Pre-Raphaelite hair.

With shining eyes, she hooked her fingers in his belt loops and tried to tug him lower, her body rising like a golden sun under his hands. She was so beautiful and so giving that his heart ached. He didn't deserve her.

Regardless, he kissed her deeply, his tongue slipping inside her mouth to lap at the sweet warmth she offered without qualm. They fell against each other, sliding halfway out of the chair, his hands tangled in her hair, their legs intertwined. Hot desire flowed like lava through Alec until every cell of his body pulsed with it, and with naked emotion and gratitude. *Thank you, thank you, thank you,* he thought, filling his arms and his mouth and his eyes with Lacey.

She laughed softly into his ear and whispered, "So, Alec, what's for dessert?"

He put his hands under her sweater and watched her face change, her eyes darkening with pleasure, before he answered.

"Hot fudge sundaes," he said. *Of course.*

8

"Vixen," he said, his mouth hot and greedy as it opened hers, his tongue stabbing, thrusting, demanding...until she was breathless and weak with wanting him.

"Vixen," he said, crushing her against his wide chest as she whimpered and clung, clawing at his shirt in her frantic need to have his skin sliding against her skin, his muscles pressing into her softness, his heart beating strongly beside hers.

"Vixen," he said, his hands pulling her hips to his so she felt the full extent of his arousal hard against her belly. She shuddered, becoming—much as she'd wanted and invited it—almost frightened by the carnal promise that emanated from him. Finally she understood: this man, with his primal need and his uncompromising body, intended to take her on the kind of dark erotic journey that would shred her gauzy schoolgirl fantasies.

Skittish or not, she craved his knowledge, his touch, his deep, obliterating thrust. She wanted to go with him. All the way.

DODGER FOLLOWED THEM upstairs. When they turned to enter the bedroom, she darted ahead, hopped onto the foot of the bed, circled three times and settled herself into a furry ball, her contented sigh daring Lacey to object.

"Let's go into my room," she whispered into Alec's ear, staking her claim with a soft bite to his lobe while they were still in Dodger's territory. The dog's ears went up, but Lacey hustled Alec along the hall and shut the door behind them. Emphatically.

She smiled at Alec's bemused expression. "I'll give Dodger my cookie, but not my man."

He put his hands on her waist. "Your man, huh?"

She put her hands on his backside. "My man."

They stood nose-to-nose, searching each other's eyes. "I think you're wearing too many clothes," Alec said at last, so Lacey stepped back and pulled her sweater off over her head.

"Not as many as you," she answered saucily. His eyes went to her breasts and the heat in both—her breasts, his eyes—made her nipples pucker beneath the thin cotton of her sleeveless undershirt. Flushed pink, she stepped on the toe of one of her loose stockings and, poised like a flamingo, slowly raised her foot until the sock stopped stretching and gave way. It wasn't a graceful maneuver, but fortunately Alec was looking only at her breasts as he distractedly unbuttoned his shirt.

"You're wearing too many clothes," she repeated, and he took off the shirt and unsnapped his trousers, his chin lowered so he stared at her from beneath dark brows drawn together.

His throat was working and his mouth shaped words without sound except for one low, provocative, ardent "...you."

Lacey flew at him. She had no breath, no thought, no intention, no control. All she had was an overpowering need to feel his arms around her, his mouth on her skin, her fingers in his hair as he came inside her, deep inside her, hot and fierce and strong. She kissed him, framing his face with her hands. "Make love to me, Alec, or I'm going to die." She pressed her thumbs into the hollows beneath his cheekbones, trying to get closer than kissing, closer than *close*. "Seriously, I'm gonna die."

He half lifted, half pushed her toward the bed. They tumbled onto it together, jarring the mattress, rolling over and around each other until she found herself pinned beneath his lithe body. He moved sinuously against her and she cried out, opening her legs so his erection could press hard against her where she needed it, rubbing through her jeans with a delicious friction, making her head swim and her fingernails sink into his smooth bare back.

"Vixen," he said, and she laughed and bit his shoulder.

He levered himself off her and pushed up her skimpy T-shirt, unhooking the bra she wore underneath with a flick of his thumb. Watching her all the while, his eyes hot on hers, he scraped his tongue across her breasts and down to her rib cage, trailing wet kisses all the way to her navel. Once there, he took the tab of her zipper between his teeth and pulled it down with one quick twist of his head, like a feral dog snapping at a bone. She gasped, her hips jerking off the bed.

He stripped off her jeans. He stripped off her tiny cotton panties. Then, his eyes still hot on hers, he stripped off the rest of his own clothes. And somehow, in doing so, he finally stripped both of them of any lingering notion that what they were doing was just having sex. It was sex—hot, wild, rampaging, jungle-beat sex—and it was more.

Lacey knew it.

Alec knew it.

But they spoke of it only with their eyes, and lips, and eager, searching hands. Suffused with pleasure, she wrapped herself around him, licking the pulsing hollow of his neck as his head reared back and he plunged into her as fiercely and deeply as she'd craved, except that the reality of having him inside her was so electric the hot shock of it went through her like a lightning bolt. When he withdrew almost all the way, she hated it, needing to be filled with him, but then he was back, sliding even deeper, and she loved it, her body clenching around his. He kept going, though. He didn't stop even when she screamed his name, clawing at him in desperation and desire. He just did it over and over and over, with her arching into his thrusts until everything in them melted and flowed and ran together, closer than close, closer than *one.*

"Oh, my goodness," Lacey said, once she found her mind and her voice, many minutes after the pressure inside her had burst into a rapture that had seemed to go on forever but of course hadn't—except for the unspoken emotions tucked away in her heart like a keepsake locket. "Darlin', I think I really did die and go to heaven." Her voice was lazy, her accent much thicker than usual.

"Did you, now?" Alec rolled over and put his arm around her. "That must mean there's an angel in my bed."

Smiling, she moved her cheek against the pillow, creeping toward the sinful promise of his mouth. "Can an angel do this?" she asked, flicking her tongue over his bottom lip, then catching it between her teeth. His mouth was fantastic—miracle-making. First thing tomorrow morning she was starting a fan club for his mouth. Dodger, Trillium and all the rest of the horses could be members, but she alone was claiming the presidency. And all the privileges of the position.

She pressed against the length of his warm, firm body. Definitely her privilege.

"Don't do that unless you mean it," he said.

She skimmed her palm over his chest, relishing how so much warm flesh and smooth muscle and sinew and bone had meshed into one beautiful male animal—a true thoroughbred. The stretch of his arm, the flex of his shoulder, the tight bead of his nipple between her teeth, the clench of his abdomen as he caught his breath—she loved all of it. All of him.

"Alec," she said with a sigh, sliding her thigh over his, bending her knee so the one loose sock that she still wore grazed his legs. He reached down and pulled off the sock, and she reached down and touched him covetously, prompting him to roll over on top of her, with his hands in her hair pinning her down and his thigh parting hers so she could feel that she'd better have meant it, she'd better be ready right now.

"Mmm, Alec," she moaned, her veins swelling and throbbing with heat. He twisted away from her, reaching for his trousers on the floor. She tilted her head back against the pillow and listened for the sound of foil tearing. "I'm so glad you came prepared," she murmured, the teasing lilt returning to her voice as she watched him through her lashes.

"That's one way of putting it."

"Keep a ready supply on hand, do you?" she asked, thinking of the farmer's daughter and the ritzy divorcée.

"One can get anything in a grocery store these days," he replied, cocking his brow at her as he rolled the condom into place. He put his hands on her breasts and squeezed lightly. "Except maybe these."

"I dunno. Let the checkout girl get a good look at you and she might volunteer—" Lacey's voice broke off. She'd lost her train of thought because Alec's mouth had fastened over her aching nipple and was kissing and licking and sucking so hard her body tried to curl in on itself, shivering with delight.

He stopped to raise his head and say, "Cold?" and she groaned as cool air washed over her dampened breast. He reached for the blue-and-white quilt they'd kicked aside and pulled it over his head, all the way up to her chin. Under the quilt his mouth found her breast and his hand went between her legs and parted her with one probing fingertip, making him say, his tongue thick against her nipple, "Hot. Definitely hot."

He touched her again, stroking inside her with a sweet, rough, driving rhythm until the heat rose to unbearable heights and finally, *finally* he moved between her thighs and up into her, and then for the rest of the night her world narrowed to only Alec and Alec's thrust and the dizzying liquid heat that flowed between them.

IN THE MORNING, Lacey was wakened by a piercing stare. Muzzy headed, she pushed her hair back from her face and pressed her temples and groaned, trying to remember how much wine she'd drunk at dinner. Two glasses. Then this must be a hangover of another sort altogether....

She licked her puffy lips and said, "I never knew sex could give a person a hangover." When there was no response from Alec, she opened her eyes, expecting to find him watching her, but his side of the bed was empty.

Well, then, who was staring?

Lacey rolled over and there was Dodger, sitting beside the bed with her head tilted and her ears cocked. A soft *grrr* reverberated in her throat.

"Morning," Lacey said, and stuck her head under the pillow.

She didn't emerge until she heard Dodger's toenails clicking out of the room and into the hall, and presumably downstairs, though one could only hope for a total retreat to the barn. Thinking *bacon*, Lacey propelled herself out of bed, letting momentum carry her all the way to the bathroom, naked as a jaybird, her hair a rat's nest. When she looked in the mirror she didn't fret over letting down Madame X's standards—she was just glad that neither Alec or Dodger was watching.

Lacey was washed and dressed and standing in the kitchen with clean teeth, combed hair and a pound of bacon before she realized that it was only 7:00 a.m. Seven o'clock! The last time she'd seen sunrise was during a modeling assignment with a photographer who had a thing about the special glow of diffused light, or some such malarkey. She was definitely a sunset kind of gal.

But Dodger was looking with interest at the bacon and she was up anyway, so... Lacey shrugged and turned in a circle, searching for the microwave. There didn't seem to be one.

She looked at the dog. "Dodger, does Daddy have a microwave?"

Apparently giving up on the bacon, Dodger walked to the door and whined to go out. "Hold on, pooch," Lacey said. "I can do this." She found a heavy, black, cast-iron skillet, the kind her grandma had used before she bought a microwave. "And just between me and you, Dodge, Grandma Lacey-Beth is nutty as a fruit-cake, so what does that say for your daddy?"

Dodger pressed her nose to the glass-paneled door.

While the bacon popped and sizzled the old-fashioned way, Lacey prowled through the house again, looking at it with a fresh eye. No computer. No fax. No television. No VCR. Naturally, no cable. However, there was a telephone—even Alec couldn't live without that—and a good stereo system, including CD player. Thanks for small favors.

She scurried back to the kitchen, remembering in the nick of time that you had to turn frying bacon. Manually. By the time the bacon was done, blotted on paper towels and set aside to cool, the smell had drawn Dodger away from the door, and Lacey was realizing that a pound of bacon was a lot for one medium-size dog, even one she was trying to bribe. She took out a carton of eggs. "Let's go for scrambled," she told the dog. "That way it won't matter how many yolks I break."

She'd crumbled two pieces of bacon into Dodger's dish—the dog skulked toward it suspiciously—and was cracking eggs into a mixing bowl when she was struck by another insight.

She hadn't thought about Mr. X or his vandalism since she'd arrived at Alec's farm. Hadn't thought about it because she felt safe.

She felt at home.

How weird was that?

ALEC CAME BACK IN TIME to turn Lacey's egg mixture into omelettes. She watched the process with some interest, thinking *hey, I could do that.* Use a no-stick pan, skip the scrambling, give a few cranks of the pepper mill and then throw in whatever cheese you pulled out of the fridge, some chopped tomatoes and peppers and feathery sprigs of green stuff… It wasn't so difficult. Perhaps knowing how to cook could come in handy. On occasion. In her opinion, doing just about anything day in, day out would get to be a grind. Unless the grind involved Alec and a bed and actual physical grinding, of course…

"What?" he said. "Why are you looking at me like that?"

She smiled mysteriously, but then canceled that out by saying, "Wanna go upstairs and do some more bodyguarding?"

Alec winced and scrubbed his hand over his face. "Look, Lacey, we've got to have a serious talk about what, uh, you know, happened last night. About…" he pointed at the ceiling… "*that.*"

"What's wrong? You can do it, but not say it?"

"I can say it."

"Well, gosh, warn me if you plan to. I'll cover Dodger's ears."

"Okay," he said through his teeth, straining to maintain his composure. "We made love. And it was—"

She beamed a sunny Marilyn at him. "Incredible."

Something in his expression showed he agreed even as he said, "I was going to explain that even though it's not the smartest thing I've ever done—"

She frowned. "Okay, *now* I'm officially insulted."

"If you'll let me finish?"

"Yes, sir." She saluted. "Whatever you say, sir."

"Considering the situation, me being your bodyguard and all, it was not—"

"Then you're fired." Her lashes fluttered. "Now can we go upstairs?"

"Lacey."

She mimed turning the key to her mouth.

Alec shook his head, but his gaze warmed as it swept over her. She blushed, thinking of how he'd stared into her eyes last night while he'd pounded inside her and she'd clenched around him. How she'd cried out, asking for more.

"I've been trying to tell you that what happened between us may have been a mistake professionally, one I'm afraid I've made before, but it was also incredible, as you said—" he nodded at her "—and I wouldn't want to stop even if I could." His brows raised slightly, and for a moment his expression was both wary and poignant, and she understood that there was a lot he wasn't saying. "So…are we okay?"

Wanting to turn cartwheels across the brick floor, she managed to contain herself to a nod. "Yup, we're okay."

"Then give me another Marilyn, will you?"

THE NEXT FOUR DAYS were practically perfect. Alec introduced Lacey to all the horses, to Peter Bellingham—who recognized her as Madame X but was sworn to silence about her visit—and to the concept of barn chores. When she said, "Yechh," Alec said that everyone who stayed at the farm had to do them. With some suspicion she asked who all was included on the visitor's list, and he admitted that only she had been so privileged up to now, which was some comfort, though not enough to make up for having to deal with horse manure on an up-close-and-personal basis.

Her false lashes were the first thing to go; the manicured nails and hot rollers soon followed. Although there was a beauty salon, the Curly Girly, in Webster Station, Alec had forbidden her to go there, claiming it was a hotbed of local gossip. Lacey was forced to clip her nails short and apply a serviceable coat of clear pol-

ish. And since her nails were plain, there didn't seem
to be much need for red lipstick—particularly when
most of it wound up smeared on Alec's face or Alec's
collar.

They couldn't go out to eat, either, not even if she
wore her disguise, because according to Alec all of
Webster Station, not just the Curly Girly, was riddled
with busybodies. In fact, he claimed that they were *famous* for their gossip. When Lacey said that she'd go
stir-crazy if she didn't get out soon, Alec started her on
horseback riding lessons to use up her energy. Which
was not what she had in mind, so finally he agreed to
an outing—a long, nighttime ride in the pickup down
winding country roads, the windows open to the crisp
autumn air and the evening sky speckled with stars,
with the radio playing something sweet and slow.
They held hands. She was content…for the time being.

It didn't take more than one swipe of horse slobber
to convince Lacey that the black velvet half of her small
wardrobe didn't suit the farm. She took to wearing
Alec's shirts and letting the horses slobber where they
would, their muzzles both prickly and soft as suede as
they snorted warm air into her palm, lipping up offer-
ings of carrots and apples and sugar cubes, rewarding
her with a swish of their tails and occasional great
foamy swipes of oat-scented slobber. Alec watched
with amusement, but kept pushing her away when she
tried to hug him after she'd been sharing confidences
with the horses.

In the evenings, they ate bowls of hot buttered pop-
corn, listened to music and played Scrabble, which
would have been extremely boring to the city Lacey if
the country Lacey hadn't invented her own rules. Once
she'd realized that Alec was one of those aggravating
persons who not only knew but actually *picked* the let-

ters for words like *twixt* and *zoysia* and *quahog*, she made up a rule that for every word he put down that was worth fifteen points or less, she would take off a piece of clothing. In essence, it was a backward version of strip Scrabble, and it led to her winning a string of very quick games. That is, until Alec made up the rule that for every word she put down that was worth more than fifteen points, *he* would take off a piece of clothing. Lacey began studying the dictionary in her spare time, which led to Alec throwing the *q* and *z* tiles into the fire when she scored big with *quetzal* and celebrated by doing a seminaked cha-cha around the living room. After that, the game degenerated into laughter and kisses and making love on the carpet in front of the fireplace.

The next morning Lacey found an *e* tile tangled in her hair and a W glued to her butt.

Yes, the days were nice, Lacey thought as she took a sheet of oatmeal cookies out of the oven. Quiet, sometimes so quiet she thought she'd go batty—witness her Betty Crocker phase—but still very nice. The nights, though…

The nights were heaven.

She pretended her blush was the result of warmth from the oven, even though there was only Dodger to notice the telltale sign of her infatuation. She gave the dog half a cookie for being discreet enough not to comment, but only half because as of this morning Alec had put Dodger on a diet. He'd said that although he was glad the dog was hanging around the kitchen and finally making friends with Lacey, the lack of exercise was showing in Dodger's roly-poly midsection.

Lacey felt guilty about that. Even though she and Dodger were sharing practically the same diet—cookies were their staple, but she had to sneak the dog a little of everything off her plate to maintain their "friend-ship"—it seemed that in usurping Alec to help her work off the calories, Lacey had left Dodger in the lurch.

But, oh, my, yes, the nights were heaven...

"Cookies again?" Alec said, coming into the kitchen to wash his hands. He was wearing his tall black boots and tight white jodhpurs and he looked good enough to eat. She could have taken bites out of his lean thighs and tight buttocks right then and there.

Instead she popped the other half of Dodger's cookie in her mouth and said, "This time I got them right." On her first attempt, she'd put in way too much baking soda and the cookies had bubbled up into one globby mass that had spread off the pan like mutant alien spore.

"Why are you looking at me like that?" Alec asked, even though by now he should know why. He must have, because he said, "Is it that thing with the jodh-purs again? I was training Rio. I had to wear them, I swear—"

Lacey laughed and wound her arms around Alec's waist from behind. It was amazing how much he'd re-laxed since they'd left Manhattan. Perhaps it was be-cause they'd given Mr. X the slip; perhaps it was be-cause they grew closer every day. Whatever the case, in many ways he was a new man. Her man. Her lover.

She hugged him tightly, transferring only one inno-cent daub of cookie batter from her blue chambray shirt to his. "All I was thinking was that we should give Dodger some exercise. What do you say, teach? Am I ready for a long horseback ride through the woods?" She was tired of riding practice circles in the schooling ring under Alec's keen eye; it was time she felt the wind in her hair.

"Sure. If you stick with Briar Rose."

Lacey stifled her groan. Briar Rose was Trillium's dam, the nicest, sweetest, tamest broodmare Alec owned. Briar Rose's lope was like a rocking chair. And as for feeling the wind in her hair...well, Lacey would likely get more action from her hair dryer.

Then again, Alec was wearing his jodhpurs, and who was she to deny herself *that* pleasure?

"Saddle 'em up," she said. "Hey, Dodge, we're going for a ride!"

"IT'S AMALIE'S FAULT," Lacey explained when Alec made her take the lead on Briar Rose so she wouldn't be distracted by his jodhpurs. "In the first *Black Velvet* book there's a fantasy involving jodhpurs that's just..." She waved her gloved hand, wordless but still expressive.

"Keep both hands on the reins," Alec instructed, thinking that he ought to read both of Amalie's books cover to cover—as a forewarning, since he probably couldn't pass off his interest as more research.

"You should read it." Lacey twisted in the saddle to look back at him. "In fact, every man on earth should read Amalie's books." She did the Marilyn. "Put this kind of smile on the face of every woman on earth."

"Turn around," he said. "You're supposed to be in charge of your mount, not distracted by inappropriate fantasies about jodhpurs, for pity's sake."

"Okay, okay," she said cheerfully. "But it's not as if Briar Rose would do anything she's not supposed to. I might as well be back home in an easy chair."

Home. Alec wondered if she realized what she'd said. Or if it meant what he hoped. Thus far he was astonished at how easily Lacey had adjusted to the quiet country life, despite her occasional colorful complaints. She had her own ways of creating excitement about everything she did, be it baking cookies or playing Scrabble.

Still, he wondered how long her contentment would last. How long before she missed being Madame X?

Dodger crashed among the underbrush, barking at mushrooms and stumps and stones while squirrels raced up the trees and rabbits shot through the thickets. A squadron of sparrows coasted on the breeze.

The scent of autumn was in the air, earthy and vital, speaking of change. Alec breathed deeply.

Had it always been like this, he wondered, or was it Lacey's presence that made the sky so sharp, the sun so warm, the color of the leaves so vivid?

"Isn't this gorgeous?" She was waving her hand again, jouncing up and down in the saddle with exuberance, her dangling earrings swinging like metronomes. They'd gone two roundabout miles along unpaved back roads and were returning via his back pasture, cresting the far side of the hill that sloped to the paddocks and barn. "Let's stop here for a while," she suggested. "To enjoy the view."

The explanation sounded unnecessary to Alec; he wondered if she had something else in mind. She almost always did, and he was almost always amenable.

They tied the horses. Dodger sat, tired but happy, her tongue lolling from her mouth. Lacey walked around for a bit, absently rubbing her backside, before she found a spot to her liking. She plopped down among the fallen leaves beneath a yellowed redbud tree. "My gosh, my legs feel like rubber bands. And here I thought using the Stairmaster and rowing machine at the gym had kept me in shape."

"Your shape is fine." Alec sat beside her, resting his arms on his upraised knees. "And you know it."

She preened for him, flipping her braid back over her shoulder and sliding one gloved hand along her dressy, as-yet-unslobbered black velvet vest. "Well, there's city shape, and then there's country shape. At some point, I hope, the two will coincide."

Which was his hope, too, although he was concerned about more than physical fitness. Compatibility, for one. Longevity, for another. Even looking back, he wasn't sure how he'd gotten to a point of such infatuation that he would be considering these things. Lacey had inserted herself into his life, even his consciousness, in both obvious and insidious ways. While she had a flair for the obvious, it turned out that her subtleties were even more engaging. For instance, although he'd come to appreciate her exultant, off-key renditions of the Lilith Fair music, he truly savored the soft humming sound she made in her sleep when he kissed her goodbye in the early mornings before heading out to the barn to feed and water the horses. So much so that he tried not to think about the day he'd have to return to sharing a bed with only Dodger and her cold nose and her intestinal problems.

"Soon I'll have been here a week." Lacey drew in a breath of the redolent air as if to fortify herself. "For days at a time I've managed to forget why I'm here. Is it possible that Mr. X has forgotten me? You know, out of sight, out of mind?"

"I wouldn't count on it."

She stripped off her gloves and scooped up a handful of crisp leaves. "I almost wish Malcolm had been the culprit."

"He was still in police custody when the break-in occurred—"

"I know." She opened her hands and bits of the

leaves fell like confetti. "Which means there's still someone out there. Waiting for Madame X."

Alec didn't want to ask, but he had to. "Are you trying to tell me that you want to go back? You haven't mentioned it in a while, so I thought maybe…"

"I can't stay forever," she said softly. The wind blew the loose tendrils of her hair across her face, obscuring her expression.

The part of Alec that was new and optimistic and buoyant, the part of him that was as much her as him, compelled him to say, "Why not?"

She tucked the loose strands of her hair behind her ears. "Why not stay?" Her eyes were an astonished and baffled blue, watching him warily, but also with hope. He hoped.

"Forever," he said.

"Y-you can't mean that."

He couldn't believe he'd said it, either. But he went on nonetheless. "We might have gotten off to a rocky start, but things have been going along pretty smoothly for us lately, haven't they?"

"But that's…" She bowed her head and was silent, scooping and crushing and scattering leaves until her folded legs were covered with them. Finally she said, her voice low and shaky, "You want only half of me, Alec." When he didn't respond, she gestured at herself. "Look at me. Boots and jeans and a chambray shirt. I haven't had my hair done since I don't know when, I'm wearing hardly any makeup, my nails are short—" she held them out and snorted "—and *dirty*. I need a facial and a manicure and…and—oh, Alec, I'm sorry, but I need to be more than just the country Lacey!"

He went cold inside. "You've been happy," he said, floundering, because where ten minutes ago that would have been a statement, it was now a question. Had she only been *acting*? Even though this time around the stakes were just one man's embattled heart and not a country's safety, had he once more been misled by a blonde with her own agenda?

Lacey stood; her arms waved dramatically. "Of course I've been happy."

"But not happy enough."

She frowned down at him. "Unlike you, I'm not ready to turn my back on the rest of the world."

He ran his hands through his hair, giving himself time to think. He'd known his relationship with Lacey would come down to this. She crackled with energy and excitement and her restless search for more, always more—of everything. It was a good part of why he'd been drawn to her, but also the very issue that would tear them apart. For a short while he'd had his kicks, taking part in Lacey's wild, tumbling, joyous journey through life, but he couldn't continue the ride, not into the sort of future she had planned for herself.

Slowly Alec got to his feet, feeling old, jaded, dispirited. He told himself that this was Lacey's nature; she had to go.

And he had to stay.

He looked at her with regret, remembering her magnificent in the firelight, stripped of all artifice, her heart in her hands. He'd been so close to a breakthrough that evening, but in the end he'd substituted making love for making peace.

My tongue will tell the anger of my heart,/Or else my heart, concealing it, will break.

"Alec," she said, her voice thick with sorrow, "surely you knew I wouldn't stay here."

He hardened himself. It would be easier to let go of her if he didn't allow emotions to complicate the matter. "Then go," he said, the words harsh and bitter in his mouth. *It's better this way*, he swore to himself, knowing he was a liar. There was no way to make this palatable.

For a moment Lacey's expression was imploring. Then her face changed and she squared her shoulders, her cheeks gone pale, her eyes sad but determined. Without a word she turned, snatched up Rio's reins and threw herself into the saddle, neglecting the stirrups as she drummed her heels against the startled horse's sides.

The black Thoroughbred made one giant leap forward and charged down the hill as if firecrackers had been set off at his heels. Lacey's exclamation of surprise was cut off in midair as her hands flew up and she made the leap forward entirely independent of the horse, landing back in the saddle with a teeth-rattling bounce. She'd lost the reins, but was able to grab Rio's mane and keep her slithering seat as the horse galloped down the hill. Dodger raced after them, barking excitedly.

Alec's heart seemed to drop from his body, leaving him hollow inside. "Lacey! Hold on!" he heard himself bellow, knowing that there was nothing else she could do, but also knowing that the white board fence at the bottom of the hill was nearly five feet high. He vaulted onto Briar Rose from the wrong side, tearing the reins free as he turned the mare on a dime and brought her to a handy gallop by sheer force of will.

Drumming hoofbeats echoed in Alec's ears. He hadn't a hope of catching up. Rio's long ebony tail streamed out from his churning hindquarters; his horseshoes and the loose, flopping irons flashed silver against the green blur of the grass. Lacey's terrified, wobbly voice rose in the sharp autumn air. "Oh-oh-oh, Alec...!"

He leaned low over Briar Rose's withers, urging her on with his voice and hands and knees and prayers. She made a valiant effort, but it wasn't nearly enough. Rio careened at breakneck speed down the hill, slowing not at all as the fence suddenly loomed before him. In perfect stride, the Thoroughbred launched himself from powerful haunches and sailed over the barricade like the winged Pegasus.

Lacey's braid whipped the air as they landed, more or less together, on the other side of the fence. She was up out of the saddle, miraculously still clinging to Rio's neck, her balance precarious until her legs clamped like pliers around the horse's ribs and she righted herself.

Alec said two words—*"Thank God"*—as Briar Rose pulled up at the fence, snorting, her hooves tearing streamers in the grass. He soothed her excitement with one hand on her lathered shoulder, drops of his own sweat running into his eyes as he turned the mare toward the gate. Dodger wiggled beneath the bottom rail of the fence.

Alec gave his forehead a quick swipe, grateful to see that Rio was slowing as he approached the barn. The horse whinnied shrilly to announce his arrival, skirting the paddocks at a rough trot that bounced Lacey in the saddle like a rag doll.

"Rein him in," Alec called, but when Rio reached the grassy forecourt of the barn, Lacey suddenly slumped. She slid from the saddle, falling to the ground in a limp, boneless heap.

9

Daniels slammed Laryssa down on the thick rug near the fireplace, jarring the breath out of her. Before she could draw another, he was on her, kissing her again, his mouth hot, so hot, so damn *hot*....

She pounded at his chest, clawed at his face, his shoulders, fighting for air and space and rational thought. He was merciless. Eyes rolling back in her head, she gave up and allowed the waves of deep, obliterating lust to take her. Instead of sinking, her body became lighter than air, suspended in a musky, miasmic heat, arching again and again toward the heavy, filling pressure forever out of its reach. Her hips rocked lasciviously.

"Please, oh, please..." Her voice detached from somewhere inside and floated up out of her mouth without decision or consent. Mindless desire had rendered her blameless. "Now...Daniels, please. I need to know. Now."

"Soon enough," he growled with his lips on her throat. He caught her breasts in his hands and rubbed hard against her swollen nipples until she felt the ache and shudder and pleasure of it boiling in her blood.

"Now!" she screamed, and he put his mouth to her ear.

"Bossy little piece, aren't you?" he whispered

as his muscled thighs pushed hers apart and he used his fingers to open her even wider. "Now," he agreed, and cleaved her with one powerful thrust.

FROM A GREAT DISTANCE she heard Alec saying her name. He sounded concerned, she thought dreamily. For reasons she couldn't remember, this eased the constriction in her chest. She felt herself growing lighter, rising toward his voice like a scuba diver following a stream of silvery bubbles through the dark sea. To salvation.

"Lacey, can you hear me?"

She blinked. "Of course I can hear you. I'm not deaf."

He pulled her into a rough embrace. "You little idiot!" He gave her shoulders a short, hard shake, then cradled her close again, one hand sliding through her hair so gently he might have been petting Dodger except that his voice continued to fire at her like a semiautomatic rifle. "Why did you try to ride Rio? Oh, man, how could you be so dumb? What in the world possessed you—"

She snuggled against his chest, strangely comforted by his bellicose concern. "I wanted to feel the wind in my hair," she murmured, although that was only half of it.

"What? Are you crazy? Don't you know that you never, never, *never* gallop a horse toward the barn? Even Briar Rose might have taken off on you. And Rio! My God, *Rio*—"

"Ah, well," she said, sighing. "There's no use shutting the barn door when the milk is free...."

Alec snorted. "Let me guess. Grandma Lacey-Beth."

"And as the milk's free, why don't we make ice

cream?'' she said, feeling stunned and sore but also rather giddy. It was true that Alec had said, "Then go," and she had, but she doubted now that he meant it. Certainly the fact of his desperation, and the feel of his arms around her, carried another message.

He held her away to examine her eyes. "Have you got a concussion?"

"Just the usual scrambled brain." Dodger nudged her way in between them and licked Lacey's chin, her tongue warm and wet, her breath hot and grassy. Lacey hugged the dog. "Oh, Dodge, you really do like me! It's not just the cookies!"

"Cookies?" Alec said, frowning.

Dodger yipped and wormed out of Lacey's arms with a careful application of hard toenails to human flesh. She trotted away with her nose in the air and her whiskers twitching. Lacey shrugged. "Well, it's a start."

"Cookies," Alec said again.

Lacey batted her lashes. "Can we get up now? This grass is not as comfortable as it could be."

He helped her stand, keeping one hand on her waist when she wobbled like a newborn foal. *"Lacey,"* he said, remembering. "Do you realize that you and Rio jumped a five-foot fence? You could have broken your neck."

"It was nothing," she said airily. "I was scared going down the hill, I admit, but Rio took that fence so cleanly it was past us before I could even think about falling off. It was almost like flying. My form was nothing to brag about, but…"

"Yeah, I know. You wanted to feel the wind in your hair."

She was beginning to comprehend how reckless she'd been. "Well, I, uh—"

"Even if you didn't care about yourself, you should have thought about the horse. Rio's green now, but one day I hope he'll be a grand prix jumper. He's worth a lot of money." Somewhat belatedly, Alec remembered that the expensive horse was still wandering around loose, and as he continued scolding Lacey for her carelessness, he caught hold of one of Rio's reins and started running his hands over the high-strung Thoroughbred's legs, checking for damage. Rio curveted in place like a figure on a music box, then settled down to chomp at a mouthful of grass, his curb chain jingling softly.

Lacey approached the tall black horse, which up close was far more formidable than she'd realized. It had been foolish, rash and just plain stupid to hop onto Rio, but she simply hadn't been thinking. When Alec had told her to leave, with his eyes gone cold and dead, her instinct had been to get away as fast as possible.

Which was still no excuse. "I'm sorry, Alec. I wasn't thinking." She held her palm flat and Rio touched it with a brush of his black velvet muzzle. His nostrils whiffled at her scent.

Alec gathered up the reins and walked Rio in a circle. "He looks okay. No harm done this time."

"There won't be a next time." They both went very still at her words, considering the possible meanings. Lacey cleared her throat. "I mean, I'll never do that again."

"I'm sorry, too," Alec said, low and fast. "I reacted badly to your…decision to leave. Of course you have to go. I just want to be sure that you're safe before you do."

Oh, Alec, she cried silently, so desperate her throat ached from holding back her need for his love. *Is that all you want?*

After a moment, she turned away to collect Briar Rose, who was waiting patiently next to the paddock. Lacey passed the reins over the mare's head, pausing briefly to blink away the tears spangling her lashes. "Good girl," she said, patting the mare's bright chestnut flank. "Guess I should've stayed with you, huh, sweetie? Even though Alec's a pretty great riding teacher, Rio's too big for my britches." She led the mare into the stable, talking endlessly to keep the rusty catch out of her voice. Still, her patter lacked its usual zip. "From now on, Briar Rose, I'm sticking to rocking chairs. Even though Grandma Lacey-Beth says an idle lap is the devil's playground."

Alec's voice came from one of the shadowed stalls, carrying an almost-normal dry inflection. "I wouldn't touch that one with a ten-foot pole."

Lacey couldn't help but grin. "If he's got a ten-foot pole, I haven't seen it," she whispered to the mare. "And believe me, darlin', I've looked."

"What's that?" Alec called.

"Just girl talk." Lacey struggled with the saddle girth. "Briar Rose has been telling me all about her love affairs. Turns out she hangs out with some real studs—oh, hi." Alec had silently crept up behind her. Despite the wild chase down the hill, he looked clean and unruffled and handsome as ever, making her remember her erotic fantasy about peeling his jodhpurs off in the hay mow with the filtered sunshine gilding his muscles and warming his eyes into pools of dark, bittersweet chocolate....

"Let me do that." With a few efficient moves, he removed the English saddle. "Are you sure you're okay?"

"I'm fine." Again she swallowed the hitch in her throat. "I think."

"You fainted...."

"Not really." She leaned against the worn oaken door of one of the stalls. The air in the stable seemed oppressive, overly rich with the scent of clean straw, fine polished leather and curried horseflesh. But, no, that wasn't it, that wasn't her problem. She was dizzy and thick and weak and dumb with wanting Alec, needing Alec, loving Alec....

"I didn't faint," she insisted. "I was, um, over-whelmed, I guess you'd say. By the time Rio slowed down, the shock of all that adrenaline—the gallop, the jump, holding on—" *losing you* "—was too much for me. I was so surprised that I was safe, I just sort of slid out of the saddle and kissed the ground in gratitude." She fanned her face. "Let's call it a case of the vapors. I am a Southern belle, you know."

"Even so, I want you to go up to the house—"

She was looking at her bare hands. "Uh-oh. I think I left my gloves at the top of the hill."

"Lacey, forget the gloves. I will get them. I will take care of the horses. You will go up to the house and re-lax. That's a direct order from your bodyguard, and for once, damn it, you will please obey it."

Her tension eased slightly. If he was back to ordering her about like a dime-store Mussolini, then things were going to be okay. She didn't see how, exactly, but there had to be a way.

"Okay." Lacey's Marilyn was weak and watery, un-worthy of its name. "At least you said please this time."

FOR FOUR-PLUS DAYS, Lacey had suppressed thoughts about her once burgeoning, now truncated career. For four-plus days, she'd resisted picking up the telephone to call Piper Hicks.

Now, with the afternoon's upsets, all her worries and conflicts had been brought to the surface. Staying with Alec, feeling cozy and safe and even loved in his arms, had been a very nice dream.

It wasn't reality.

It could be, though, if they both worked to make it so. But Lacey didn't see that happening. She wasn't going to trash her ambition because Alec had problems with it. She wasn't going to deny the Madame X side of herself so he could keep her down on the farm.

She went into the living room and gingerly sat at the rolltop desk, every muscle in her thighs and buttocks making their protest known. She needed a warm bath very badly, but only half as much as she needed to re-establish connections with her agent.

Deliberately disregarding Alec's instructions forbidding it, Lacey reached for the phone.

One teeny-weeny call wouldn't hurt.

HALF AN HOUR LATER, Lacey was still soaking in the bathtub when Alec knocked at the bathroom door. She had purposely left it open a crack in silent invitation, but hadn't expected that he would knock first. She'd believed they'd gone beyond knocking, though perhaps after today they were back at square one.

She thought guiltily of her conversation with Piper Hicks. After keeping Lacey waiting on hold, Piper had finally consented to take the call. She'd been cool but professional, as briskly efficient as ever, and Lacey had taken some comfort in knowing that at least she hadn't been dropped as a client. Yet. Apparently Piper had cleared the Madame X schedule only up to this weekend. On Saturday, there was a *Black Velvet*-inspired charity fashion show that could not be canceled. Madame X's participation was the show's centerpiece, and Piper had said that she expected Lacey to be there—no two ways about it. It was show-or-go time.

Although logically Lacey knew she shouldn't hesitate—her livelihood was at stake, after all—she couldn't quite bring herself to commit, for one simple, yet frightfully complicated reason: she didn't want to leave Alec. Unaccustomed to such indecision, she'd gone upstairs to sulk in the bathtub.

"Hey," she said softly when Alec knocked and then glanced inside. She pushed her hands through the warm, silky water, making ripples. "Come in, Alec. Don't worry, I'm indecent."

That brought him up short, even though he'd already stepped inside. She sank a little lower in the tub to make up for the fact that there were no bubbles in her bath. Not that it helped. All it meant was that she was now nude below the clear, faintly amber tinged water instead of above it.

"This can wait," Alec said, holding up a thick manila envelope.

"No, please come talk to me. Look…" She placed a soaked washcloth over her breasts. "Now I'm decent."

He hesitated. "Not exactly." There were tiny stars of interest shining in the dark pools of his eyes.

She brought up her knees. "Don't be shy. You've seen it all anyway." She flashed a smile. "Not only seen it. You've *touched* it." Her shoulders shimmied, playfully seductive. "Oh, my, yes, how you've touched it…."

Alec tried to look away and couldn't. He tried not to return her smile and couldn't prevent that, either. Helplessly, hopelessly charmed, he told himself that he should have expected that she'd rebound quicker than Michael Jordan. Nothing kept Lacey Longwood down for long. In fact, fifteen minutes after she left Alec she'd probably have a new boyfriend.

A shot of pain ricocheted through him, followed by a bolt from the blue: *he would not give her up.*

How this could be accomplished was immaterial at the moment. All he knew was that he'd given up on too much in his life. Lacey would not be included on the list.

Feeling almost light-headed—it was too soon to call it relief—he pulled a wicker step stool over to the tub and sat and looked at Lacey with wonder. And, inevitably, desire. She was limpid eyed and dewy skinned from the warm bath, her disheveled hair slipping from a clip to hang in dampened ringlets against her neck. Beneath the water she was all golden curves and graceful limbs, a sea creature like no other. He swore he felt his heart expanding, pounding blood through his swelling veins until he was as engorged as a fatted calf.

"What's this?" Lacey asked, sliding sideways through the water to reach for Alec's packet of photos. She rested her wet arms on the lip of the tub, her breasts pressed full and round against the porcelain. An already impressive cleavage deepened as she ripped open the envelope and shook out its contents. "Well, well. Photos from Lil Wingo."

"Uh...I thought they might help us...." Alec searched his fogged brain. *Get a grip, Danieli.* "They might give us a clue to help identify Mr. X."

"I see." Pulling on her lip, she flipped through the photos and contact sheets, mostly taken at her various *Black Velvet* events. "Did you think a certain maniacal gleam in the eye would tell us which onlooker is my dear, demented correspondent?"

"I'm clutching at straws here." He put out one hand,

his fingers closing around the edge of the tub, his thumb just barely grazing Lacey's upper arm.

Carelessly she shoved the photos into the envelope. Her head turned, and she fleetingly pressed her cheek against his hand. She brushed a soft kiss across his white knuckles.

He started to reach for her, but she moved away, settling her shoulders against the slope of porcelain as she carefully readjusted the washcloth, which covered only enough to be titillating. "I'll be downstairs in a minute or two," she promised. "We can go through the photos then."

"Right," Alec said. "Right." He walked stiffly to the door, silently vowing that he absolutely wasn't giving up Lacey.

Nothing could be righter.

IT WAS MORE THAN A MINUTE or two before they reconvened. Alec went out to the stable to take care of the horses for the night, then came back and showered and changed into another black turtleneck and pressed chinos cinched with a narrow, black leather belt. Lacey hadn't seen the need to dress again after her bath; she wore one of her extravagant black velvet robes over nothing but perfumed skin.

They danced around each other in the kitchen, scrupulously polite, saying little. Alec offered to make pasta. Lacey wanted only a salad. She was starting a new diet, although just for tonight she didn't want to think about why.

After grazing on sprouts and lettuce, she wandered into the living room while Alec did the dishes. The packet of photos was on the coffee table, but the sight of it made her sigh. She turned away, idly rubbing the rich, sensuous velvet of her robe between two fingers.

She went to the sound system that Alec had set up in an old, darkened pine armoire. Choosing *Fumbling toward Ecstasy* for its title, she slipped the disc into the CD player. As the music swelled, a secretive, catlike smile sprang to her face. She had an idea. A deliciously wicked, terribly fattening idea.

Ah, well. She'd start her diet tomorrow.

LACEY SAILED into the kitchen, the quilted lapels of her robe pulled up high so the black velvet framed her fresh skin and blond ringlets like a portrait of some queen or other that Alec had once seen at the Victoria and Albert Museum in London.

"I'm in charge of dessert tonight," she said with a sly sideways glance. "Would you go and light the fire? I have a treat in store for you."

He was agreeable. Where Lacey was concerned, he'd come to see, he was becoming more and more agreeable all the time. "And don't you touch the music," she called after him.

Absorbed with thoughts of Lacey—Lacey leaving, Lacey staying—he raked the coals and arranged a neat stack of birch logs. After setting a match to the kindling and closing the screen, he had nothing to do but sit back and wait. He patiently did so through several soul-searching Lilith Fair–type numbers about love and pain and ecstasy. When Lacey finally arrived, she was bearing a tray filled with a round carton of French vanilla ice cream, spoons, a jar of cherries, a can of whipping cream and a silver dish of what looked like hot fudge.

Alec turned a suspicious eye on her, suspecting that she'd divined her secret nickname. She smiled, giving away nothing. He glanced again at the tray. "Nice," he said, "but you forgot the bowls."

"No, I didn't." She knelt on the rug, her back to the brick fireplace, and spread a tablecloth on the floor.

"No bowls?"

"We won't be needing bowls."

He watched as she slowly stirred the hot fudge, lifting the spoon higher and higher above the dish, making the rich, dark topping swirl and flow in ways that were almost sensual.

Alec swallowed uneasily. "Why..." he started to ask, when without ceremony Lacey slipped the velvet robe off her shoulders and drizzled a spoonful of hot fudge over her bare breasts. His mouth dropped open. "Oh. I see."

The thick, warm liquid glistened on her skin; she seemed to swoon under its effect. "Mmm," she purred, rubbing her lips together. "You asked why?" One fingertip traced through the fudge topping. "Listen to the lyrics of this song, Alec."

He tried to concentrate, he really did, but how could he when Lacey was sitting half-naked before him with glossy streaks of fudge slowly slipping down the curves of her breasts? He could barely remember to breathe, let alone decipher any messages from the music.

One of her fingers flicked beneath her nipple to catch a droplet of the satiny fudge. Absently licking her finger clean, she peered into the carton of softened ice cream. She dug a scoop into it, then with a flutter of her lashes and a teasing smile, picked up the can of whipping cream.

It struck Alec as absurd. He even might have laughed if he could have pried his tongue off the roof of his mouth. Did she really expect him to...?

She did. She stretched out flat on the tablecloth and scooped a dollop of ice cream into the hollow between

her breasts. He closed his eyes and finally realized that
Sarah McLachlan—why had he ever said anything bad
about Lilith Fair?—was singing to a lover, swearing
that their love was better than ice cream, better than
chocolate, better than anything....

At that, Alec's eyes popped open. Quite a statement
for the Goddess of Hot Fudge Sundaes to have chosen
to illustrate.

Did she mean it, or was this just another *Black Velvet*
fantasy? And why hadn't he read those books through
when he'd had the chance?

"Alec, sweetie," she crooned. "I'm melting...."

"The things you come up with," he said, sounding
stunned as he hovered above her on his hands and
knees. "You don't seriously expect..." He glanced
again at her glistening breasts. "I'm not the kind of guy
who can..."

Laughing, Lacey brandished the can of whipping
cream. She tilted back her head and squirted a foamy
shot of it onto her extended tongue. Alec watched,
astonished, unmoving. With her hand on the back of
his neck, she drew him lower and kissed him, her
tongue lathered with cream. He made a soft, moaning
sound and opened his mouth to hers, taking in both
her and the cream in one long, sucking pull. Their ensuing kiss was slow, sensuous, unbearably sweet.

Alec pulled away. "You got hot fudge all over
my—"

"Take it off."

He gave her a hot, fiery look, and stripped off the
turtleneck. When his head emerged, she was lavishly
squirting whipping cream over each of her hot-fudge-
smeared breasts and the scoop of melting ice cream
placed between them. The contrast of cold and warm

made her bare skin shiver and tingle, though in truth she found it more silly and ticklish than erotic.

She giggled. "Hey, Alec, did you ever see that famous album cover with the girl sitting in a mountain of whipping cream?" The ice cream was liquefying into the fudge, pooling between her breasts and running down her sides. This fantasy was a messy one.

"I don't know." Alec framed his hands around her hot-fudge-sundae breasts, perhaps to contain the drips...perhaps not. "I can't think..."

She reached over to the tray, using her fingers to scoop up a couple of the long-stemmed cherries.

His brows scrunched together. "Lacey?" He sat back on his heels. "You're not going to..."

"Why not?" She plopped the cherries in place, handed him a spoon and laid her head down on the tablecloth, smiling brilliantly at his quandary. "Okay, Alec, dig in. Dessert's on me."

In the end, he didn't use the spoon. She couldn't even say that he got to eat much of his dessert, because most of it was squashed between them in a slippery, gloppy mess when finally Alec surrendered with a muttered oath and took her by the shoulders, pulled her against his bare chest and kissed her for such a long while that her brain melted into a sweet, sappy goo, not unlike the ice cream, which had by that time dripped into every crease and crevice of her body. Still disbelieving, yet obviously turned on despite himself, Alec wonderingly slid his palms over her breasts and midriff and back again, then down to her belly and hips and again to her breasts, painting her with the fudgy liquid until her torso looked like a hand-dipped chocolate Easter bunny.

Glistening in the firelight, she rose to her knees and slipped out of the wraparound velvet robe, carelessly letting it crumple beneath her on the tablecloth. Alec stared. She closed her eyes—his were too intense to meet—and ran her hands over her breasts and arms and thighs while the sweetly aching need grew sharper and sharper, until she had to squirm against her own caresses, desperate for release.

Gently Alec pushed her to the floor. His mouth locked on each of her breasts in turn, sucking off the thin coating of cream and fudge, lapping with broad strokes of his tongue, licking her painfully tight nipples until her breasts were shiny and clean.

He wasn't finished, though. His hands traveled lower, along the soft curve of her belly, the flare of her hip, the warm flesh of her parted thighs. One of his fingers traced along the crease where thigh met groin, dislodging something soft and squishy. With a soft chuckle, he brought up his hand so she could see the long-stemmed cherry dangling from his fingertips.

Holding her eyes with his, he brushed it across her lips, then lifted it to his own and deliberately, devilishly crunched it between his white teeth. "Alec," she breathed, emotion catching at her throat again as she rose to her elbows and kissed him, the cherry's pink juice running over their lips and probing tongues as they searched, savored, swallowed.... It was sweet, so sweet, but not nearly enough. She had to have more.

Alec panted against her skin as he stroked his tongue down the center of her body—between her breasts, bisecting her rib cage, into her navel, over her belly and going still lower, her stomach muscles jumping and her hips arching to meet the ecstasy as his mouth fastened between her open legs and his tongue dipped inside her, licking as though she were an ice-cream cone. When she cried out and tried to roll away because it was too good, too much, he put his hand on her stomach and held her in place, his mouth hot, his tongue clever, parting her, probing her, penetrating with deep, sucking strokes until the stark pleasure and sweet pressure of it spilled over inside her and she came in screaming, shivering spasms against his mouth.

In her blissful state, Lacey thought she might have lost consciousness, but from a distance she felt Alec kissing her, slowly making his way up the length of her sticky body. "Okay, enough is enough," he said, and sprang up, catching her hand.

"Wait," she said, thinking of how she could use the fudge sauce on *him*. But he herded her to her feet—she was about as limp and compliant as he was ever going to get her—insisting, "Forget about it, goddess. We're taking a shower."

Which sounded sort of nice to her, but she looked down at his fudge-stained chinos and asked, "What about you?" as she pressed her palm against his thick arousal. "You've been neglected."

"Delayed gratification," he said through his teeth, and took her hand away.

What impressive self-control, she thought only minutes later, standing in the claw-foot tub while Alec, nude now himself and still semierect, soaped her up. As this wasn't a night for half measures, she took the soap away and pushed him out of the spray of water and up against the wall. "Your turn."

"I'm already clean," he protested, then shut his mouth when she slowly slid the soap over his chest. It was startlingly erotic, with her fingernails tracing designs on his prickling skin and her slippery body pressing into his. He groaned with pleasure.

She lost the soap after a while and used only her hands on him, the ministrations becoming more intimate as she stroked and squeezed until he was gasping, his blood surging with primitive instincts, his pulsing erection grown larger and hotter and needier than should have been possible. He stepped under the showerhead, thinking that the lukewarm water would cool him off, but it didn't. Lacey was pressed to his backside, reaching around....

"Quit that," he said.

"You don't really want me to," she purred, and since she was right, he threw back the shower curtain and lifted her bodily from the tub, not caring about the water splashing everywhere or even stopping for towels as he carried the Goddess of Hot Fudge Sundaes through the hallway to the bedroom and threw her down on the tarnished brass bed and climbed on top of her even before she'd stopped bouncing. Luckily, there were still a few condom packets scattered on the floor by the bed or he wouldn't have remembered those, either, but there were, and he did, sheathing himself even as he parted her thighs and slid easily into her, their wet bodies fitting like a jigsaw puzzle, so attuned they found each other's rhythm by instinct and swiftly rode the pounding tempo of their lovemaking into a crushing oblivion.

ONLY AN HOUR LATER, maybe two, Alec woke Lacey up. Although they had air-dried, the bed beneath them was damp, too clammy and uncomfortable to sleep in. Lacey complained, but he herded her to her feet again and pointed her toward his bedroom. Wrapped in a wrinkled sheet, she shuffled along like a little old lady, wads of tangled hair falling into her sleepy eyes. He thought she'd never been more beautiful.

They reached his stark tan-and-ivory bedroom. Dodger must have found another place to sleep, for they had the room all to themselves. Lacey dropped the damp sheet, rubbed her eyes and then glanced, blinking, at her well-loved body. "And to think you used to hate me," she said dreamily.

"Never," he said. "Not hate. I was leery of trusting you, perhaps...."

Her eyes sharpened, but then she yawned and slumped onto the bed. Flushed with unaccustomed tenderness, he helped her to get comfortable, tucking the clean sheets and thick comforter around her. Thanking the heavens that she was still with him, that he had been fortunate enough to find her in the first place and that now they were here *together*, he climbed into bed beside her and fitted his body around hers. She sighed sweetly, clasped her hands over his and promptly fell asleep.

He waited for several minutes to be sure. Then he touched his lips to her shoulder and said, "Her name was Ecaterina Szako."

Lacey stirred slightly, then resettled with another soft sigh. Calling himself a coward for not facing up to his past in the harsh light of day, Alec continued in a husky whisper. "I'd been assigned to a...special project in Zhabekistan. We knew an insurrection was brewing, one that could put the capital city and its coastline up for grabs. Cat was an interpreter, working at the embassy. She was beautiful and charming. And, as it turned out, so very much more."

He stopped. Lacey's body was soft in his arms; her breathing pattern continued as before, even and uninterrupted.

He closed his eyes. "Later we learned that Cat was born illegitimately of a Russian mother and a Romanian father. She'd been one of the Soviet Union's infamous femme fatale spies, trained in language and diplomacy, seduction and subterfuge. Fortunately, I wasn't completely taken in...." *Only enough to dull my edge.*

"But others were," he whispered. "And I was responsible."

Unconsciously, Alec's arms tightened around Lacey as he remembered the siege on the embassy and the staccato report of M-16 fire in the night, the devastating court-martial of two young sergeants from the marine security guard. He remembered Cat's notoriety, and his own, and his request for an honorable discharge that had felt in every way dishonorable.

"I suppose so," Lacey murmured.

Alec winced in surprise, then narrowed his eyes, straining to see her face in the dark. He detected a slight quiver of her dusky lashes against the curve of her cheek. "Pardon?" he said, his jaw clenching.

She stirred. "I suppose you were responsible."

He squeezed his eyes shut, then opened them again. "Yes. That's what I said."

"I mean..." she turned in his arms "...you were with those guards every moment of the day, and all night long, too, weren't you? You followed them when they were off duty, and you even crawled inside their minds and questioned their every thought and decision, right?" Her fingertips rested lightly on his arm. "Well, gosh, Alec, if you did all that, then obviously you were responsible for every single mistake they made."

His throat tightened. "You don't understand."

"Probably not. Just like Jericho didn't understand when he wrote those articles clearing your name."

"I shouldn't have been in a position to need my name cleared in the first place."

"Oh, Alec..." Lacey leaned her forehead against his

chest and, God help him, he felt his eyes welling up at the breadth and depth of his love for her. How had such a thing happened, when he'd once sworn with all that was in him that he would never get emotionally involved again?

"Let me ask you this, then," she said. "Am I responsible for Mr. X? Is it my fault he's such a creep? If he...*gets* me, will you say, 'Too bad, but she should've never put on that black velvet in the first place'?"

In truth, Alec would have been just as glad if she never again wore black velvet for anyone but him. He had to admit he saw her point. "Okay." He sighed, the guilt that weighed on him easing up the tiniest bit. *"Okay."*

Lacey snuggled into him, her lips pressing stamps of approval on his shoulder, his collarbone, his chest. "So. What happened to this Cat person? Something truly rotten, I hope?"

For once, he didn't freeze up at the name. "She's locked up in a Zhabekistani jail. The conditions there probably qualify as truly rotten."

"Hmm. And you actually thought I was the same type of woman as her?" Lacey's nails bit lightly into his arm in warning. "I'm absolutely appalled."

"I didn't..." He stopped and shook his head at his stupidity. "I did. But only briefly. Only superficially."

She laughed softly. "Okay. I can forgive you for that. People *have* been known to make the mistake of believing that I'm no more than the sum of my parts."

"It's a mighty impressive sum...." He reached out his hand.

She wiggled one of her parts into it. "But not the total. *Remember that.*"

Before he bent his head to hers, Alec made her a promise, bittersweet though it was. "I could never forget a single thing about you, Lacey Longwood. Like it or not, you're burned into my heart forever."

10

Laryssa was on fire.

With his first lunge, Daniels had opened a searing, jagged core of white-hot pleasure through the center of her; every subsequent thrust stoked the fire hotter and hotter.

Her blood screamed with heat. His touch sizzled on her skin. Desire seethed like molten lava from her, fusing the joining of their bodies in flame.

Her silly, spoiled attempts at girlish flirtation had burned up and floated away like ashes on the wind. What was left was passion—pure, adult, blatant, consuming. She sobbed with it as he put his hands under her hips and lifted her to meet the hot, pulsing arrow of his penetration, her body tightening like a bowstring, arching into his filling heat, both of them slick with sweat, shining in the flickering light, wild untamed creatures born of fire and desire and ravening need.

On fire, she was on fire—burning up from the inside out…!

EVERYTHING HAD CHANGED, and nothing had changed.

They were easier with each other, closer and more assured of their mutual regard, but not yet fully committed. So much still stood between them—not the least of which was Mr. X.

And Madame X, too, Lacey admitted.

Yawning, she picked up the rather disgusting remains of the past evening's feast. Somehow, one never considered in advance how to handle the less romantic, more humbling aspects of the aftermath of a fantasy-turned-reality. Clucking over just how much of the hot fudge she'd managed to drizzle out of the dish and over, well, *everything,* she dropped the sticky silver into the sink and dumped the rest of the contents of the tray into the trash. The tablecloth could be washed, but the black velvet robe would definitely have to go to the dry cleaner's.

She glanced at a pocket-size calendar stuck to the fridge. It was Friday. Tomorrow evening was the *Black Velvet* fashion show. How was she going to tell Alec that she had to go—if not today, then tomorrow morning at the latest?

How would he react?

For that matter, how would *she* react—especially if he forbade her to leave?

Alec had moved the packet of Lil Wingo's photographs to the kitchen table. Lacey thought that she'd rather muck out stalls than search faces in crowds for a maniac, but it was a task she could no longer put off. Particularly if she intended to return to Manhattan as Madame X.

She had the photos spread over the table when Alec came in from the barn. "You're up early," he said, going to the sink to wash his hands, as was his habit.

"Farm life's a bad influence on me."

He came over and kissed the top of her head. He brushed her arms with a gentle caress, and fleetingly she caught his hands in hers, tangling their fingers in a lover's knot. It was the sort of moment with the power to turn Lacey's heart to mush. She'd known plenty of guys who wanted to make love to her, not so many who also wanted simply to love her.

Trust a marine to come through, she thought. Semper fi, and all that.

Alec moved away. "Have you had breakfast?"

"I'll get some yogurt later." No more bacon and eggs until she'd shed eight pounds. "Why don't you come over here and go through these photos with me? I don't know what I'm supposed to be looking for."

Without being asked, he brought her a dish of plain yogurt topped with granola and banana slices. What a guy.

He sat and peeled a banana for himself. "Mainly, we want to identify any person who's shown up at more than one event, which could tip us off to someone who's developed an unhealthy interest in you."

She flipped through a few of the photos doubtfully. "I'm afraid Madame X has more than her share of Malcolm O'Brians."

"Fine. Point them out to me. Malcolm was a good candidate for Mr. X, just not *the* candidate, as it turned out."

"What if Mr. X is not a mister?"

Alec shook his head. "Those letters weren't written by a woman."

"How can you be sure? Maybe it was a woman trying to sound like a man to camouflage her identity."

"Did you have someone in mind?"

"Well, no, but..." She picked up a sheaf of recent photographs, ones Lil had taken at the publicity event for *All That Glitters.* "How about Bobbie Brandolini? She thinks I stole her thunder on the soap opera, and look at this." Lacey pointed to a snapshot that had caught Bobbie staring daggers at Lacey behind her back. "Judging by the look on her face, I think she must despise me."

Alec examined the picture as he finished the banana. "This is the actress with the foul mouth, the one who plays...?"

"Ashleigh. Ashleigh was in a car accident, remember, and it's touch and go whether or not the writers are going to kill her off. My character, Velvet Valancy, was very popular, and when I return...well, who knows? Bobbie might not want to chance that Ashleigh's coma will become permanent."

"Maybe," Alec said, contemplating the variables. He tapped the table. "It fits that Bobbie might want to scare you off, but not actually hurt you." He thought of the vandalism at the book signing and shook his head. "Nope, it doesn't feel right. Bobbie only wants you off the show. She has no reason to keep you from the rest of your career as Madame X. Think of the handcuffs, the word *vixen*. That's what's significant."

Ill at ease, Lacey stirred the yogurt, filled her spoon, then let it plop back into the bowl. "You know, the handcuffs seem to remind me of something...." Even with her eyes closed she could feel Alec watching her closely. His gaze still had the power to scramble her thought processes, but she tried to blank him out and concentrate on the elusive memory. Finally she shook her head. "I don't know. I can't put my finger on it."

"Something someone said?" he prodded. "Something from one of the books—"

"Don't push me!" she said tartly, then told herself to stop and take a deep breath. Alec was showing natural concern; he was not trying to take over her life. She was still the captain of her own ship, even though it resembled the *Titanic*—big and gaudy and going down fast.

"If it's important, it'll come to me. Without anyone's guidance."

To his credit, Alec backed off. "Okay. You're right." He looked resigned. "It'll come to you." But he also looked worried.

They went through every single photograph, but made little progress, to Lacey's way of thinking. At Alec's insistence, she identified each of her acquaintances and business associates and the few fans she knew by name or face. They even considered the photographers, the booksellers, the various security guards and hospitality escorts who'd danced attendance on Madame X. By the time they were through, Lacey was almost ready to turn in her black velvet uniform and retire to the farm.

He was relentless. While she was dragging, suffering from eyestrain and Sahara tongue, he efficiently arranged Lil's photos in chronological order, ready to go at the Mr. X problem from another direction.

"I'd forgotten how relentless marines can be," she said, searching the fridge for bottled water. Oh, horror, there was none; she'd have to drink from the tap.

"Pardon?"

"Marines. Relentless. Single-minded." She sucked down a liter-size glass of water in several huge swallows. "Gung ho."

He cocked an eyebrow. "You've had experience?"

"You mean other than you?" She wiped her mouth and grinned. "Actually, I have. You forget I grew up in South Carolina. Nice girls were warned to steer clear of the Parris Island area—which meant that of course I had to see what was what. I dated a few marines when I was eighteen or nineteen and still too dumb to know better." She laughed at his expression, a melange of hubris, insult, alarm and jealousy. "Shame we didn't run into each other."

"Just as well," he muttered. "I'd've broken training for the likes of you."

"How did you get to be a marine, anyway? I've been wondering about that." But she hadn't wanted to ask him when bringing up the subject meant being frozen out. At least that had finally changed.

He shrugged. "I told you that my father was in foreign service, assigned to various overseas embassies. He sent me to good schools, hoping I'd be interested in international law, languages, diplomacy, that kind of thing."

"But you weren't?"

"I had two interests when I was young. Horses, and the MSG—marine security guard—who protect the embassies and their personnel. This was around the time when there began to be a lot of terrorist activity. To a kid, wearing suits and greeting diplomats at stuffy receptions seemed pretty damn dull in comparison."

"I see. You know, that's sort of how I came to feel about dressing up in sequins and sashes and performing 'Summertime' for the millionth time versus jetting off to St. Bart's with a string bikini and a French photographer."

Alec's eyebrows shot halfway up his forehead. "I don't know which is more dangerous an assignment."

Lacey laughed knowingly. "Oh, I do."

"I don't want to hear the details." He started flipping through the photos again. "French, huh?" He shook his head; a lock of blue-black hair fell over his furrowed brow. "Why do they always have to be French?"

She patted his hand. "Don't take it so hard. Half the time they're gay."

He looked at her without blinking. "Shall we get back to the photographs?"

She laughed. "All right. But I don't see what good this will do. Nothing new is going to show up." She plucked the top photograph off the pile. "This is a shot taken at my very first appearance as Madame X, a publisher's party way back when the people at Pebblepond Press thought I truly was Madame X. There's Norris Yount, Rosie Bass and my agent at the time—"

"Let's focus on him." Alec glanced at his notes. "Bennett Cooper."

"I already told you. He was smart and slick, but also kind of lazy, and not all that helpful to my career. Even the Madame X thing was something that Amalie and I cooked up between us." Lacey stopped, suddenly concerned, and looked under the table. "Say, have you seen Dodger this morning? She's usually begging for her midmorning cookie around now."

"She's probably outside," Alec said offhandedly, still concentrating on Lacey's ex-agent. "You said Cooper was angry when you signed with Piper Hicks."

She sat back, stretching her arms overhead. "Well, of course. He thought he had me locked into a long-term contract, but Piper's legal team found some loophole or other...."

Alec's eyes glittered. "Sounds like motive to me."

"Don't get too excited." She rubbed her neck. "Bennett got over it. He even showed up at my apartment on moving day, bringing flowers and offering to help out. He carried those papier-mâché trees up to my new—"

The doorbell rang. "Hold that thought," Alec said, and went to answer it.

When he came back, the look on his face made Lacey's skin rise into goose bumps. "You gave Piper Hicks this address," he accused.

Her heartbeat stuttered. "I did not—"

"Don't try to deceive me." He tossed a slim cardboard envelope from an overnight delivery service onto the tabletop. "There's the proof."

Fingers shaking, she grabbed up the envelope and read the address, then the return address: Piper Hicks, Inc. *Oh, rats.* "Look, Alec, I didn't intend…" She shot a glance at his face and swallowed the rest of her denials. "Okay. I called, yes, but I swear I only told Piper that I was staying with a friend. I did not give her your address. I don't know how she…"

"It's easy enough to get an address if you've got a telephone number."

"I didn't give that, either!"

"They probably have a system that automatically records the numbers of incoming calls. Which is why I told you not to telephone *anyone*, including your agent and your best friend and your grandma Lacey-Beth." He stopped, breathing hard, and negligently flipped the envelope out of her hands with a flick of one finger. "This could have easily been a delivery from Mr. X instead of your agent. Do you get it now?"

When Lacey tried to nod, her head jerked like a marionette with a broken string. "I get it. But how long did you think you could keep me here, incommunicado?"

Alec's voice ground like crushed glass. "Until you're safe."

"Sure," she whispered. "Whenever that would be." Her voice rose. "What *you* don't get is that I can't wait here forever while the rest of my life dissolves into nothing. I can't—" she stood to face Alec full on

"—and I won't. I won't let some creep with a Madame X complex control my actions!"

He stared right back at her. "Are you referring to me or Mr. X?"

She silently replayed her last words, then gave a short, flustered laugh, her throat unclenching. "Oh! Of course not *you*. I mean, uh, even though you do try to control me, you're certainly not a creep...."

"Glad to hear it."

Weak-kneed, she slithered into her chair. She was in no shape to walk out on Alec. Although she did intend to go back to her "real" life, she wanted to do it with his support, his encouragement, his love. Was that too much to ask?

"As long as I'm making confessions," she said, reaching for the delivery from Piper, tearing the cardboard open, "I might as well tell you that there's a *Black Velvet* fashion show in Manhattan tomorrow evening. I have to be there—it's for charity, and they've advertised and sold tickets...." She slid her finger under the flap of a flat inner envelope and pulled out a certificate, not the fashion show schedule she'd halfway expected. "This is strange."

At once Alec was at her side. "What is it?"

A silent shriek filled Lacey's head. She was holding a death certificate.

Her own.

"IT'S A HIGH-QUALITY laser copy," Alec said after he'd examined the death certificate under a strong light. "All he had to do was type in your personal information in the proper blanks. It looks very official, but it's meaningless."

"Meaningless?" Lacey said. Her face was chalky. "The message in the letter is very pointed."

Madame X's correspondent had been succinct for once. "You're better off dead," read the note that had accompanied the death certificate. "See that you stay that way, vixen."

"I think," Alec said carefully, "that we could take this as a good sign. Mr. X doesn't seem to want you truly dead. He only wants you to stop being Madame X."

"Well, isn't that super?" Lacey shot to her feet and strode around the kitchen, her arms wrapped around herself. "We've found something you two can agree on."

"That's not fair, Lacey."

"I know." Her lips tightened. "I'm just upset. I felt so safe here, so…at home. And now Mr. X has invaded even this place with his filth. By overnight mail, of all things!"

Which was pretty significant, Alec thought. All along he'd been betting that the suspect—the *creep*—was an acquaintance of Lacey's. As of this morning, his money had been on Bennett Cooper, the ex-agent. But now…

Lacey halted by the back door. "How did he get this address?" Her eyes narrowed. "And why was Piper Hicks, Inc. used as the return address? Do you think…" She shuddered. "Was it my telephone call?"

"It seems likely," Alec said. No use buffering what was plain as day.

Lacey groaned. "Go ahead and say it. You told me so."

He took no pleasure in being right. "There are two possibilities. Either Mr. X works at Piper's agency, or he has an in with one of her employees. Obviously someone there was waiting for your call."

"The call went through a switchboard," Lacey said

excitedly. "I talked to a receptionist, then Piper's secretary, then Piper. If we eliminate Piper from suspicion, that leaves—"

"Not so fast. We have no way of knowing who any of these people talked to, or what their connections are, or how—"

"Then you're saying that Mr. X could still be *anyone*." Lacey waved toward the window showing the wide green lawn, the brick stable, the brilliant blaze of deciduous trees covering the hillsides. "He could be anywhere. He could be out there right now. He could even be inside, hiding in a closet, for all we know, couldn't he?"

Alec wrapped his arms around her. "No. You're safe. He's not here, I promise. You're safe."

She hugged him as tightly as she held herself under control. She seemed to want his comfort, but was also just as determined not to collapse in his arms and let him soothe away her worries. "You can't guarantee my safety, Alec." Her eyes sought his. "No one can. Not even me."

"We can take precautions. Such as canceling your appearance at that fashion-show thing you mentioned."

She stepped out of his arms. "And then what? Cancel my role on *All That Glitters?*" Her usually lovely contralto was grated, strained, worried, yet also full of a kind of brash conviction that made Alec fearful. He knew she was scrappy and courageous, but being so now would put her at too much risk.

She was shaking her head. "I won't do that. I say we make a stand. Show him that I am absolutely *not* dead in any meaning of the word."

"Lacey, no." He wouldn't let her go. "I'm telling you no."

She waved him off. A strange expression passed over her face. "Alec, where's Dodger?"

This time the question got through to him. Where *was* Dodger?

"Alec," Lacey said again, her eyes wide with alarm. "Don't even think it."

"Then where is she? Have you seen her this morning?"

He moved swiftly through the house, calling Dodger's name. The dog hadn't accompanied him to the stable as she normally did. She hadn't been in her usual spot on his bed last night, either.

"Dodger?" Lacey warbled, rattling the bag she'd grabbed in the kitchen. "I've got cookies...."

A weak whimper came from the living room. "Dodger?" Alec said, searching the room. He spotted the dog lying flat on her side under the rolltop desk. She had scarcely enough strength to lift her head off the floor.

"Dodger?" Alec got down on hands and knees and tried to coax the dog to come out, but she only whimpered and laid down her head. She panted heavily, tongue slipping limply from the side of her mouth. "Dodger, girl, what's wrong?"

"She's been sick," Lacey said, sniffing at an unpleasant, sweetish sour odor rising from a corner of the room.

"Poison?" Alec wondered aloud, reaching toward his pet. Dodger's tail waved slightly, and he rested his hand on the rapid rise and fall of her chest. Not poison. Not Dodger. Not another failure of his duty.

Warily, Lacey glanced into the corner. "It was the fudge," she said suddenly, jubilantly. "She's sick from eating fudge, not poison!"

"Fudge *is* poison to a dog." Alec patted Dodger's

shoulder, his own gone slack with relief. If they got her to the vet in a hurry, she would be okay. And Lacey was safe—for now.

He was still in the game.

LACEY FELT GUILTY about leaving the dish of fudge sauce on the floor, and she felt guilty about insisting that she must go back to New York for the fashion show. They discussed it heatedly in the pickup on the way to the vet's, with Lacey cradling Dodger in her arms. If Dodger—poor, sick, stinky, sticky Dodger— wasn't her friend after this…well, then, she'd simply have to try harder.

She'd wanted to stay home and start calling airlines, but Alec wouldn't let her. He pointed out that if she'd believed for even a second that Mr. X could have somehow managed to poison Dodger, then it was foolhardy to take the same chance with her own life. She said that she'd have to be on her own at some point in her journey back to the city, and he said that if she insisted on going, damn it, then he'd go with her! They left it at that for the time being.

The vet said that, yep, Dodger had consumed a dangerous amount of the hot fudge topping, but she was going to be okay. Lacey breathed a sigh of relief. She knew that she was often too much woman for even the most confident of men, but she'd never imagined a dog bearing the brunt of her…appetite. From now on, she decided, no more fantasies involving food. Considering her problems with Mr. X, it might be a good idea to say no more fantasies, period.

But that was what he wanted—for her to be muted, stifled, repressed, controlled. Silent as the grave.

If she wouldn't do that for Alec, she certainly wouldn't for Mr. X.

She was who she was.

They'd just have to deal with it.

"I never knew it could be like that," Laryssa said to the man who was her chauffeur, her part-time bodyguard...and her brand-new lover. An all-purpose employee, she thought smugly, someone to service her every need. All women should have one.

The fire had died down to a pile of searing red embers, the kind that needed only stirring to encourage another conflagration. Not unlike the two of them, she recognized with an immense amount of self-congratulations. A small, witchy smile played across her lips.

"Normally it's not," Daniels said, stroking her hip with a proprietary laziness. She expected he'd earned that right...for the time being.

They'd moved to her massive, four-poster, king-size bed. She rolled onto her back and gazed up at the peach silk canopy with complete satisfaction. "I was marvelous," she said. "The best you've ever had, I imagine."

Daniels's laugh was cavalier, perhaps dismissive. "My, my, still such a spoiled little vixen. Have you learned nothing?"

Her eyes narrowed speculatively. Then the taunting smile reappeared as she fluidly twined herself around Daniels, rubbing against him like a kitten. "What are you going to do about it?" she challenged, sticking out her impertinent little chin.

He flipped her onto her back and pressed his hard, heavy body into hers. "Shall I demonstrate again?"

She sank her nails into his shoulders. "Go on and try it, Daniels." She laughed; it was what they both wanted. "You just try to tame me."

LACEY SPENT the next afternoon penned up in a luxurious hotel room, and she didn't like it. It was a compromise, she tried to tell herself. She shouldn't complain.

She and Alec had taken a train into New York early that morning—another compromise, since she'd wanted to fly, but he'd said that the shorter her stay in the city the better. Now, while Alec was out consulting with the fashion show's security force and asking probing questions at Piper Hicks, Inc., Lacey was stuck away in a cell—albeit a posh cell. She felt like a very precious and breakable china doll, the kind that her mother had once given her for Christmas and then forbade her to play with.

It was incredibly boring.

Lacey started going through the photographs again, not expecting to find anything. And she didn't. Just the faces of admiring fans, her own painted mug beaming out at the crowds, various shoulder-to-shoulder line-ups of "important" personages, half of whom seemed to be looking down her cleavage.

She pushed the photos away and lay flat on the bed, her arms outflung. There was nothing to do. She couldn't even call room service because Alec had told her not to.

She crossed her wrists over her head. He might as well have handcuffed her, as he'd joked he'd do if she misbehaved. A bad joke, under the circumstances, but both of them had been tense, their nerves stretched taut in anticipation of Mr. X's next move.

Handcuffs, Lacey thought. Why had he left the handcuffs?

The letters popped into her head. Not the ones Alec had read but the two she'd received among her soap opera fan mail, the two she'd read once and then thrown away.

There had been a phrase in one of the letters that reminded her of the handcuffs...something about being chained together for life. An unbreakable union. No escape.

That was it!

She sat up, scrambling among the stack of photos and scattered sections of the *New York Express* for the beeper that Alec had left with her for emergencies.

SOMEWHAT RELUCTANTLY, Piper Hicks had granted Alec access to her office staff. She was appalled that he would intimate any connection between one of her employees and the Madame X stalker. He held his tongue about his suspicions, stressing only that he wanted to discover how the delivery had been made under the agency's good name.

The receptionist who normally handled incoming calls was not at work that day. Alec asked to interview Piper's personal secretary, a woman so impeccably groomed that it was easy to overlook how plain, almost homely, she was. In her tight chignon and expensive designer suit, Kimberley Moss was a very self-possessed young lady.

She responded carefully to each of Alec's questions, stopping to think for a moment before answering, revealing no special feelings toward Lacey either as a client or as a woman. "I'm sure she's a fine person," Kimberley said. She brushed at a nonexistent speck on her lapel and lightly touched one fingertip to her pearl earring. "It has been my pleasure to work with Ms. Longwood."

"Do you remember taking her call two days ago?"

Kimberley's thin lips pursed for just a millisecond. "Certainly. I'm afraid she was put on hold for several minutes. Mrs. Hicks was on another line."

"Were you curious about the origination of Lacey's call?"

"Not particularly." The secretary brushed her fist along the side of her neck, her knuckles buffeting the earring. "Although..." She hesitated, contemplating her answer. "Mrs. Hicks has been agitated about Ms. Longwood's disappearance. I had to cancel several of the *Black Velvet* appearances we'd scheduled. It was bothersome."

"For you? Or for Mrs. Hicks?"

Kimberley almost smiled. "Whatever affects Mrs. Hicks affects me. However, I was the one who handled the cancellations. Mrs. Hicks extended personal apologies to all concerned, of course."

"The agency's telecommunication system records the numbers of all incoming calls," Alec observed sharply.

Kimberley stiffened. "Yes."

"You have access to these records?"

She fiddled with the pearl earring. "I can't imagine why I'd need them."

Alec let the point go. He smiled warmly at the secretary, prompting a peachy color to flare in her hollow cheeks. She turned and rested her fingertips on the keyboard of her computer terminal. Her sleek brown head tilted toward him. "If you're finished, Mr. Danieli?"

The beeper went off in his pocket. He took it out, checked the message and started to reach for the telephone on Kimberley Moss's desk. "May I?"

"Certainly, sir."

"Alec, I've got it," Lacey said as soon as his call was forwarded to her hotel room. "Bennett Cooper is Mr. X. He has to be!"

"What makes you say that?"

"I remembered about the handcuffs. They must refer to my contract with Bennett—the one Piper broke so I could sign with her. It was all in one of the letters I threw away. The unbreakable union—"

"Slow down," Alec said. "What unbreakable union?"

Kimberley Moss darted a glance at him.

Lacey's voice spilled from the telephone. "That's what it said in the letter. Don't you see? He must be angry about losing his percentage of my career earnings. Making nice to me on moving day with flowers and all was just a cover! Plus, I've been looking through Lil's photos and guess what? There's Bennett Cooper, plain as day, attending some of the events even *after* he was no longer my agent. He's got to be Mr. X! D'you think we can have him arrested?"

"I don't know," Alec said carefully, trying to watch the secretary's responses without seeming to.

Lacey sighed gustily. "Well, really, I must say you don't sound very enthused."

"It's best to take this slowly." Deliberately, he added, "We're not ready to arrest anyone yet." Kimberley tensed. "There are still questions that must be answered."

"Rats," Lacey said. "I've got to get out of this hotel room."

"Do not move. I'll be there straightaway." With a glance at the secretary, he disconnected the call, punched out a series of random numbers to defeat the redial button, then replaced the receiver. "Thanks, Kimberley. If you don't mind that I call you Kimberley?"

She dropped her chin, not looking at him. "I don't mind, Mr. Danieli."

"And I'm Alec," he said. "Was there something you wanted to say, Kimberley? I noticed your reaction...."

Again she hesitated, rubbing her pinkie behind her ear. "No, sir."

"You're certain?" he coaxed.

She shook her head, then spoke anyway. "It was that phrase you used. 'Unbreakable union.' It made me think you were speaking to Mrs. Hicks, but of course you weren't."

A chill went down Alec's spine. "Mrs. Hicks uses the same phrase?"

Kimberley darted a glance at her employer's closed office door. "She has something against marriage. Against divorce, to be more precise. She likes to say that the courts have seen fit to render no union unbreakable, which is tough luck for middle-aged women but very profitable for Piper Hicks, Inc."

Interesting, Alec thought, trying to fit this new information beside Lacey's discovery. He looked at Kimberley Moss, weighing the likelihood that she was hiding a motive. There was a way, he believed, to test her veracity. "You're loyal to Mrs. Hicks, aren't you, Kimberley?" he asked suddenly.

The secretary's head snapped up. "Absolutely."

Alec waited, unblinking.

After a moment of silent tension, clearly unable to stop herself, Kimberley Moss reached up and touched her pearl earring.

IT WAS WITH A SENSE of foreboding that Alec and Lacey arrived at the bustling scene of the charity fashion show. An old, shabbily elegant off-Broadway theater had been converted for the event. A new runway projected from the stage proper, its make-do plywood-and-post construction concealed by extravagant swags of black velvet and strings of fairy lights.

Stagehands were testing the glitzy spotlights, flicking them on and off, bathing Lacey's face in a changing pattern of rainbow light as she stopped in the middle of the stage to survey the activity. "Wow," she said. "I wish Amalie was here to see this."

Alec tried to hustle her away. "Let's go find your dressing room." The open area of the stage felt too exposed even without the audience in place. How would it be once the theater was dark and all eyes were on the models?

He thought uneasily of Lacey taking her turn on the catwalk—alone and vulnerable. But she refused to cancel, and aside from keeping the ushers and security guards on alert, it seemed that he'd run out of options...except for one far-fetched idea that he'd rather not have to attempt.

An officious little potbellied man in a velour tracksuit swooped in on Lacey. "Madame X! We've been waiting for you!" He rose to his tiptoes and waved his clipboard like a policeman directing traffic. "Move aside, gentlemen! This way, please, Madame X. I've arranged everything as your people requested."

"My people?" Lacey said under her breath to Alec as they walked through the backstage area.

"I dropped your name and wielded your influence with impunity," he admitted. "Madame X is quite the phenomenon."

"The elevator is a bit tricky," their escort said apologetically. He ushered them into it and pulled the iron gate. "The better dressing rooms are on the lower levels, if you don't mind the bumpy ride."

"I love rickety elevators." Lacey smiled, using the sway of the elevator to bump her hip against Alec's. "So does my bodyguard. We find them very stimulating."

"Really? How unusual." Mr. Clipboard turned to Alec, taking him to be the more practical of the two. "Here's your ID and backstage passes. We'll need Madame X in the costume room for her final fitting in— oh, let's say—" He glanced at his wristwatch.

Alec interrupted. "Madame X will be in her dressing room. Your people can come to her."

"But we don't—"

"No argument. That's how it is. And I'll be checking IDs at the door."

They'd walked down a narrow corridor and arrived at a door with a sign that read MADAME X fastened on with Scotch tape. The escort opened the door with a flourish. "Here we are." He did a magic-wand wave with his clipboard, but the tiny dressing room's faded paint and dingy furnishings weren't transformed. "Flowers, champagne, fruit basket," the show director said importantly. "Full star treatment."

Alec ripped the sign off the door. He held out his hand, palm up, and requested, "Keys. Show schedule. Security system and floor plans." Mr. Clipboard surrendered most of the pages from his clipboard and was briskly shown the door. "Thank you," Alec said. "Goodbye."

"My gosh, Alec." Lacey waved her arms. "You realize you're giving me a reputation here? Tomorrow the gossip columns will be full of how Madame X has turned into a nasty, spoiled diva whom no one can stand to work with. A real vixen, shall we say."

He was not concerned about her reputation. "It's just for tonight. Soon, I hope, Mr. X will not be a problem."

"Then you agree it's Bennett Cooper?"

Even though that solution made a lot of sense, Alec still had his reservations. Mainly because of what Kimberley Moss had said about Piper Hicks. As it was also possible that the secretary had been intentionally misleading him, he'd decided to limit his suspicions about Piper to himself and the security force for the time being.

"We might as well go over our security procedures," he said. Lacey crinkled her nose. "Now, I've given the ushers and guards photos of Bennett Cooper. If he tries to get in, they'll detain him. That doesn't mean you're safe, though, so stay on your toes. Cooper could wear a disguise as easily as you did." He flipped through the papers until he came to a photocopy of the theater's floor plans. "Furthermore, you're not to leave this room. I'm going to stay with you, and I'll answer the door and check IDs of anyone who needs to get in. Pretend you *are* a spoiled diva. Sit back and do nothing."

"That's not very inspiring." She glanced around the small room, her hands on her hips. "You want me to do *nothing*, huh? Like the girls in horror flicks who stand and scream while the killer attacks them."

Alec tried out a tight smile. "If someone actually attacks, you can respond appropriately."

Her eyes rolled. "Thanks for permission."

"Just don't be like the girls in the horror flicks who

hear a creak in the attic and go up to investigate wearing a bra and panties."

Lacey burst into genuine laughter. "Okay, that's a deal." As the room, at Alec's direction, had been stripped of everything except a low, narrow sofa, the dressing table and one chair—even the closet door had been taken off its hinges—she started investigating her stash of celebrity goodies. There were several liters of designer bottled water, a box of chocolates, the aforementioned fruit basket and flower arrangement. The pièce de résistance, as far as Lacey was concerned, was the magnum of imported French champagne. *Très magnifique!* She *loved* the star treatment!

"A bit of the bubbly?" she asked Alec, bringing the bottle and two crystal flutes over to the dressing table.

He was wearing his game face—alert, stoic, strictly business. "Save it for when we can celebrate you making it through this show in one piece."

Delayed gratification, she thought with a sigh. "Spoken like a true bodyguard."

"For now, that's what I am. *All* I am."

He was positioned at the door as though he expected an armored tank to come crashing through. No doubt he could stop one, if need be.

But could he resist one determined diva? She went over and slid her hand along the placket of his charcoal oxford-cloth shirt. His suit was black, loose fitting, expensive, made of raw silk. Not as sensuous as velvet, but she could make do.

Alec's collar was open; she touched her lips to the hollow of his throat and felt him swallow. She tipped his chin up on her fingertips and drew her tongue over his throat, the underside of his clean-shaven jaw. She made a nibbling pass across his chin. His burnt-tobacco eyes smoldered.

"This is not appropriate," he said, and put his hands on her fanny.

"I know. That's why I like it."

"We can't—"

"Just one kiss to tide me over?"

"Temptress." He was smiling as he brought his lips in line with hers. She smiled, too, and lightly pressed her mouth onto his, opening it just a little so she could take his sensual lower lip between hers, running her tongue over it, opening wider to suckle gently, pleasure humming in her throat.

Alec's fingertips caressed her face before sinking into her hair. "I love that sound you make." He tilted her head and deepened the kiss, slowly, luxuriously, as if they had all the time in the world.

Someone knocked, rattling the flimsy door on its hinges.

Alec dropped Lacey like a hot potato, his eyes gone hard. "Who is it?"

"Wardrobe."

He found the clipboard and checked that the woman's ID matched his information on her, then inspected the garment and accessory bags she carried before allowing her into the room.

Lacey glanced through her outfits. "That's all there is?"

"I've cut your turns to two," Alec said. "I don't want you going out there any more than necessary."

She sighed heavily, but held her tongue. When she started changing into the first dress, the woman from wardrobe glanced at Alec expectantly. He colored slightly and turned away.

"My goodness," Lacey said, once she'd changed and was staring at herself in the mirror while the other woman fussed over the garment's fit and length. "Oh, my gosh. Look at me."

Alec obliged. His eyes widened. "You're not wearing that."

The outfit, such as it was, consisted of black velvet undergarments and a three-hankies-and-a-promise peekaboo-black-lace overdress. Lacey twirled. "I think it's a kick."

"But everyone will be looking at you."

She blew him a kiss. "That's the point, darlin'."

He narrowed his eyes. "Including Mr. X."

Lacey hesitated for a moment. "Well, yes, but I doubt Mr. X plans to pick me off the catwalk with a rifle." She faked a laugh, hoping that Alec would laugh with her.

He did not. Instead he said, very solemnly, "Who knows what he'll try?"

Her heart felt as heavy as a brick. "You don't really think that's possible!"

"It's not likely, but…" He continued to stare at her, emotions warring in his eyes. Suddenly his expression cleared, as if he'd finally made a difficult decision. "That's it," he said. "I'm going with you."

Lacey brushed past the kneeling wardrobe mistress as she approached Alec, everything in her focused on his words. For a moment her lips moved in silence before she found her voice. "Going with me…?"

"Out on stage."

She couldn't have been more shocked if an armored tank *had* busted through the dressing room door. "You don't want to do that, Alec," she said, grateful, oh, yes, eternally grateful, but certain she should refuse. "Think of the cameras.…"

"I don't care about the cameras."

"You may be recognized."

"I know." He winced almost imperceptibly. "And I know what they'll say. 'Disgraced Marine Escorts Black Velvet Vixen.' I don't care about that, either."

Lacey rushed into his arms, crushing several layers of the lace handkerchief dress between them. The wardrobe mistress made concerned sounds, but they did not notice. They were kissing, tumultuous kisses filled with passion and fire and a newborn emotion that was nonetheless stronger than all their others combined. "Why?" Lacey whispered, her fingertips flickering over his brow, his eyes, his lips, alighting, then fluttering elsewhere, every touch filled with wonderment and awe that he would sacrifice his precious privacy for her. *"Why?"*

"You should know." His powerful eyes engaged hers even as he gave a negligent, self-effacing shrug. She felt the deep heat of his response rising in him, spilling over. "Because I love you, of course."

Her heart swooned. "Of course," she said, suddenly laughing, her eyes glittering with happiness and tears.

He put his mouth to her ear. "It's the hot fudge sundaes. I'm addicted."

She wound her arms around him and held on tight, filled with a magnificent, surging sense of joy. "And of course you know that I feel the same way. I love you, too."

He hugged the breath out of her, his eyes as clear as the Virginia night sky, his slow-breaking smile freed at last of its bitter constraints. "Of course," he said. "Of course."

The wardrobe mistress cleared her throat. "Ma'am? The dress?" Lacey and Alec were otherwise occupied. "Ma'am—sir—I'm sorry, but you're wrinkling the dress. I have to ask you to…" She stopped. They didn't. She shrugged and stepped from the room. "I'll just go and get an ironing board, then, sir, if that's okay?" They still didn't hear her. "Okay," she said, and closed the door.

IN THE END, the *Black Velvet* fashion show was completed without incident. Alec wore his own black silk suit for his and Lacey's first appearance on the runway. He hesitated for a moment backstage when he heard the loud music and louder applause, but she took his hand, flashed him the Marilyn and swung into her supermodel strut. What could he do but follow a woman like that—to the ends of the earth, if need be?

Their second appearance closed the show to rousing applause. Lacey had changed into spike heels and a long, slinky, black velvet number with a bodice laced so tightly she was almost overflowing its confines. The wardrobe people stripped a black velvet frock coat off one of the male models and quickly ripped out a few seams to fit it to Alec's shoulders. He felt like a dandy when they added a velvet string tie, but it was too late to bow out. He was committed.

Between the spotlights and the flashbulbs, he couldn't make out individual faces in the crowd. Praying that the guards at the doors had done their jobs, he escorted Lacey to the end of the catwalk and stood to one side while she did a showy, undulant turn and posed for a moment, blowing kisses to the raucous audience. Alec looked at her and forgot what the cameras were doing to his exile from the world. It no longer mattered what the press might say about him in tomorrow's papers. He had Lacey, and the knowledge that he had, after all, done his best for his country. That was enough.

"THE SECRETARY HAD A TELL," Alec said to Lacey once they were finally alone in the dressing room, after negotiating the backstage crush of hugs and congratulations and "Where *have* you been?" exclamations.

He said a firm goodbye to a lingering well-wisher and locked the door. "Every time Kimberley Moss lied to me, she touched her earring. I think it's very possible that she's Bennett Cooper's link to your new agency. She seemed susceptible to flattery, and you did say Cooper's a smooth talker."

"So that's how he found out I was in Virginia, from when I called Piper at the agency." Lacey breathed a sigh of relief that the fashion show had been completed safely, and that perhaps she'd soon be free of her stalker, as well. "And that's how he was able to deliver the death certificate under the agency's name."

"We still have no proof of any of this," Alec reminded her. "Besides, the secretary also said something to me that seemed to hint Piper Hicks could be involved."

Lacey laughed in disbelief. "Not Piper! She's much too refined."

"Remember the unbreakable union thing? Has Piper ever used that phrase around you, in reference to the contract of marriage?"

Lacey tried to think back, even though her brain was still spinning. So much had happened that day it was tough to concentrate. "Well, no," she finally said, "but Piper has mentioned her divorce a few times, in a jaded, ironic way. Really, though, Alec—Piper? Piper wouldn't—"

"She was at the book signing. She has access to all your personal information. She knew you were in New Jersey the night of the break-in."

Lacey shook her head. "I've been wondering about that break-in, how you said there was no damage to my locks. What if Bennett took my keys when I was moving out of my old apartment into the new one, and then made a copy of them? He was there all day, lifting and carrying things, going in and out, running errands—which was very unlike him even when he was still my agent. He could have stopped at a one-hour key place during one of the trips between apartments...."

Alec paced the small dressing room, following his own train of thought. "Piper could be twisted enough to hate you for breaking your original contract with Bennett Cooper, even if she was the one to instigate it. Or maybe her husband left her for a young, beautiful blonde."

"This is ridiculous, Alec." Lacey went to him and lovingly smoothed the lapels of his black velvet frock coat. "We can discuss this until the sun comes up or we can break open that bottle of champagne and celebrate your debut as a fashion model." She kissed his cheek. "Hmm? Which would you rather?"

He slipped out of the coat, letting it fall to the floor. "Thanks, but there are better things to celebrate. Like this, for instance...." He started unlacing her bodice, since she was spilling out of it anyway.

There was a frantic pounding at the door. "Mr. Danieli—we have a problem with security! Someone's spotted your man!"

Alec rushed to the door, but had the presence of mind to take precautions before he opened it. Once he'd confirmed that the alert was serious, he turned back to Lacey. "Stay here. Don't move. I'm going to check this out. It's probably a false alarm, but I'm leaving this guard outside your door to be safe."

"All right." Lacey touched his face, nervously aware

for the first time that he'd been wearing a shoulder holster under his coat. "Be careful."

"Don't open this door to anyone but me." He kissed her once, hard, and was gone before she could beg him to stay with her. Not for her own safety, but for his.

She exchanged a worried look with the security guard and started to close the door. Suddenly Piper Hicks appeared before her, done up as usual in diamond rings and ancient Chanel. "Lacey, dear, I've been looking for you."

Struck with a sudden chill, Lacey resisted the urge to slam the door in her agent's face. She didn't believe that Piper was Mr. X, not for a moment. The very idea was laughable, but, strangely, Lacey no longer felt like laughing. "Piper," she said around the lump in her throat. She glanced at the guard. "I'm sorry, but now's not the best time..."

"Nonsense. I haven't seen you in a week. We have business to discuss." Piper glanced up and down the narrow corridor. Someone was wheeling a rack full of the evening's black velvet apparel toward them. "And I'd rather not do this in the hallway," she concluded, her thin eyebrows arching higher and higher at every second of Lacey's hesitation.

"I'm sorry," Lacey said again. "I can't—"

Whoever was pushing the rack of clothing couldn't see where it was going and bumped into Piper. Lacey put out her hand to steady the older woman. The security guard stepped behind them and all three did an awkward minuet, bumping into each other, before the guard gave the rack a shove back the way it had come, clearing the doorway to the dressing room.

Lacey still felt funny about letting the agent into her room when Alec had warned her not to. Then again,

Piper was too small and fragile to do anyone harm, even if she *had* gone off her rocker.

Piper solved the problem by shooting her cuffs and marching into the dressing room. Lacey followed, deciding that she'd leave the door open.

It thudded shut the instant she stepped inside. The lock clicked as Lacey whirled, fear rising in her throat. *Bennett Cooper.* He'd been hiding behind the door! She opened her mouth to scream.

Bennett lunged at her, putting a knife to her neck. "Don't make a sound," he hissed. "Or I'll have to cut you."

A tight laugh gurgled in Lacey's throat. "Pretty bad dialogue, don'tcha think, Bennett?" She tried to sound unconcerned. Bennett Cooper was tall and well put together, but he was also lazy and unathletic. If there hadn't been a knife aimed at her jugular, sapping her spunk, she believed she could have taken him.

Piper tucked her purse under her arm and walked toward the door. "This is insupportable," she said, her voice as snippy as a scissors. "I won't stand for it."

Bennett dragged Lacey over to block the way. "Sit down, Mrs. Hicks." He chuckled and pressed the blade of the knife against Lacey's skin, drawing a bead of blood. "It's a surprise to have you here, but I am so pleased that we meet again."

Piper did not answer, though she sank onto the dressing-table chair, her thin nostrils fluttering in outrage.

Lacey took a deep, shuddering breath. The trickle of blood making its way down her throat had riveted her turbulent thoughts to only one. *Escape.* She must stay calm and stall Bennett until she could think of a way out.

She licked her lips. "I know y-you're not really going

to hurt us, Bennett, so what's the point? What are you trying to prove?"

"I don't give a damn about proving anything," he sneered, tightening his hold on her. "All I want is what you two have cheated me of."

"Money. You want money?"

"I'd be on my way to becoming a rich, influential man if you hadn't broken that contract, *Madame X*."

"Contracts are made to be broken," Piper said bitterly. "That's the way of the world."

Bennett reeked of nervousness; his hand felt sweaty on Lacey's wrist. If she could twist out of his grasp—

Suddenly the knife flashed past her ear. Piper gasped as a large hank of Lacey's hair fell to the floor. "Don't try anything," Bennett warned. "I'll cut you, I swear it."

Lacey abandoned her plan. He was more proficient with the knife than she'd expected. Frantically, her gaze darted around the dressing room, searching for help. She identified no possible weapons except the heavy champagne bottle and the corkscrew that lay beside it, within Piper's reach. Lacey tried to catch her agent's eye.

Piper was defiant, though unmoving, holding her gaze so steadily on Bennett it made him more and more nervous. "Conniving bitch," he seethed, panting in Lacey's ear. He twisted her arm. "Vixen."

She swallowed. "If—if you j-just want money from me, why try to end my career?" Like a blessing from above, she suddenly remembered the beeper that Alec had given her. He'd told her to keep it with her even during the fashion show, so she'd put it somewhere handy, but out of the way.

The beeper was in her bra.

"Scared you good, huh, vixen?" Bennett laughed. "It

was no more than you deserved. Too bad you don't know when to quit."

Slowly Lacey slid her free hand up over her tight bodice. Thank God Alec had begun to unlace her. Hoping to distract her captor, she said, "You've got to leave now, Bennett, before my bodyguard comes back. It's your only chance to get away."

Piper started to slip off her diamond rings, a far better distraction. "Take them and go," she said. She unclipped her heavy gold-and-pearl earrings and added them to the pile. Lacey felt Bennett straining to look over her shoulder, his greed engaged by the small stash of expensive jewelry.

When Piper removed her gold Piaget watch, Lacey took a chance and dipped her fingers into her cleavage to find the beeper. "What are you doing?" Bennett growled, and she caught her breath, pressing her hand to her chest in a helpless feminine gesture.

"My heart's just beatin' so fast," she said, praying she'd pressed the right button on the beeper and that Alec was on his way. "I must be gettin' the vapors."

"Shut up." Bennett's gaze was drawn from Lacey's cleavage back to the jewelry.

Piper removed her ruby brooch. "That's everything—every piece of jewelry my swine of an ex ever gave me. You're welcome to it, Cooper Bennett, and good riddance, I must say."

Bennett hesitated for a long moment. Lacey didn't dare to breathe.

"Cut your losses," Piper advised dryly.

Bennett must have realized he was in a no-win situation, because suddenly he pushed Lacey violently away from himself, sending her crashing into Piper. The chair collapsed beneath the two women, spilling them to the floor.

The door crashed open. Bennett froze for a split second, his hands filled with Piper's diamonds and gold, and that was long enough for both Alec and Lacey to act.

Alec struck low, taking one long stride into the room and launching himself at Bennett's legs as the man turned to slash the knife through thin air. Lacey had leaped to her feet and snatched up the champagne bottle. She swung wildly, missing Bennett's head entirely. The bottle slammed down hard onto his shoulder, making his arm jerk involuntarily. He howled in pain and dropped the knife.

Bennett's head snapped back as Alec reached up and jerked the agent off his feet. At the same moment, Lacey brought the bottle down on his forehead with a tremendous, shattering smash. Champagne gushed over all three of them as Bennett Cooper fell unconscious to the floor, his eyeballs rolling back in their sockets.

"Alec!" Lacey went down on her knees amid the puddle of champagne and broken glass, desperate to know that he wasn't hurt.

Alec rolled out from beneath Bennett's dead weight. "I'm all right. Watch out for the glass. Damn. Was that Dom Perignon?"

Too choked up to answer, Lacey threw her arms around him, knocking them both back to the floor as she covered his face with kisses. After a while, he gave up trying to stand.

Piper had recovered from her fall. She tottered to the dressing table, giving a wide berth to the melodramatic lovers and the mess on the floor, and retrieved her jewels one by one. "Contracts may be broken, but diamonds are a girl's best friend," she said to no one in particular, and turned to leave as security guards flooded the room.

"So IT WAS BENNETT COOPER, after all."

Lacey nodded. "He'd heard Piper's theory on the advantages of *breakable unions* during their contract tussle." She tried to wring out the damp, heavy fabric of her velvet dress. "You know, Alec, I didn't let him into the room on purpose. Or Piper, either. It just sort of happened." She didn't explain about how Bennett had hidden behind the rack of designer duds. Done in by black velvet dresses! She'd never hear the end of it.

"Was he just crazy," Alec wondered, "or was there a method to his madness?"

"I think at first he wanted only to ruin my career as Madame X, since he felt cheated of the profits. When that didn't work..." She shrugged. "Maybe he just started to hate me."

Alec looked out over the empty theater. "'My tongue will tell the anger of my heart,/Or else my heart, concealing it, will break.'"

Lacey gave him a wan smile, feeling bedraggled with her wet dress and unevenly chopped hair. "Is it time for this shrew to be tamed?"

Alec's eyes glittered in the footlights as he looked at her and smiled a smile that matched her Marilyn tooth for tooth. "Are you kidding? I wouldn't want my shrew any other way." He laughed and swept her up in his arms. Almost, anyway; Lacey's toes dangled two whole inches above the stage.

They kissed, sweetly, tenderly, gratefully. Alec pressed his face against Lacey's throat, his lips finding the tiny cut made by Bennett's knife. She felt him shudder.

"It's okay," she whispered. "We're both safe and sound."

He murmured in agreement. She ran her fingers

through his shaggy hair and kissed his forehead. "I love you, Alec. So much."

"I love you. Even more." His tongue licked across the slope of her breasts experimentally. "Mmm. You taste like champagne."

"First time I ever took a shower in it. What a waste of an excellent vintage."

Alec licked her again. "Maybe not," he said with wicked intent.

She suppressed her laugh. "Forget the champagne, will you?"

He set her down and took her face in his hands. "I'll buy you a case of champagne, a hundred cases. For our wedding. And a diamond, too."

"I do believe I'll hold you to that," she said, glowing. She thought of how she'd grown to appreciate farm life, how she could split her time between Virginia and New York, and how maybe that meant she'd only have to take the jobs she really wanted. And she thought of how none of those things were what was most significant.

She kissed Alec again. "Actually, darlin', the diamond's not important as long as I've got you. 'Cause you're a hero, you know? A true hero."

Because she believed it, so did he. And that was good enough, and strong enough, to last a lifetime.

Reverently, he slid his palms over her flamboyant curves. "And you, woman, are one hell of a black velvet vixen."

He's strong. He's sexy.
He's up for grabs!

Harlequin Temptation and
Texas Men magazine present:

1998 Mail Order Men

#691 THE LONE WOLF
by Sandy Steen—July 1998

#695 SINGLE IN THE SADDLE
by Vicki Lewis Thompson—August 1998

#699 SINGLE SHERIFF SEEKS...
by Jo Leigh—September 1998

#703 STILL HITCHED, COWBOY
by Leandra Logan—October 1998

#707 TALL, DARK AND RECKLESS
by Lyn Ellis—November 1998

#711 MR. DECEMBER
by Heather MacAllister—December 1998

Mail Order Men—
Satisfaction Guaranteed!

Available wherever Harlequin books are sold.

MEN at WORK

All work and no play?
Not these men!

October 1998
SOUND OF SUMMER by Annette Broadrick
Secret agent Adam Conroy's seductive gaze
could hypnotize a woman's heart. But it was
Selena Stanford's body that needed saving—
when she stumbled into the middle of an
espionage ring and forced Adam out of
hiding....

November 1998
GLASS HOUSES by Anne Stuart
Billionaire Michael Dubrovnik never lost a
negotiation—until Laura de Kelsey Winston
changed the boardroom rules. He might
acquire her business...but a kiss would cost
him his heart....

December 1998
FIT TO BE TIED by Joan Johnston
Matthew Benson had a way with words
and women—but he refused to be tied
down. Could Jennifer Smith get him to
retract his scathing review of her art by
trying another tactic: tying him *up*?

Available at your favorite retail outlet!

MEN AT WORK™

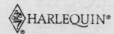 

Mysterious, sexy, sizzling...

THE AUSTRALIANS

Stories of romance Australian-style, guaranteed to
fulfill that sense of adventure!

This November look for
Borrowed—One Bride
by **Trisha David**

Beth Lister is surprised when Kell Hallam kidnaps her on her
wedding day and takes her to his dusty ranch, Coolbuma. Just
who is Kell, and what is his mysterious plan? But Beth is even
more surprised when passion begins to rise between her and
her captor!

*The Wonder from Down Under: where spirited women win
the hearts of Australia's most independent men!*

Available November 1998
where books are sold.

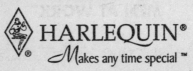

HARLEQUIN®
Makes any time special ™

WHEN THINGS START TO HEAT UP
HIRE A BODYGUARD...

YOUR BODY IS OUR BUSINESS
Discreet, professional
protection

1-800-555-HERO

AND THEN IT GETS HOTTER!

There's a bodyguard agency in San Francisco where
you can always find a HERO FOR HIRE, and the man
of your sexiest fantasies.... Five of your favorite
Temptation authors have just been there:

JOANN ROSS *1-800-HERO*
August 1998
KATE HOFFMANN *A BODY TO DIE FOR*
September 1998
PATRICIA RYAN *IN HOT PURSUIT*
October 1998
MARGARET BROWNLEY *BODY LANGUAGE*
November 1998
RUTH JEAN DALE *A PRIVATE EYEFUL*
December 1998

HERO FOR HIRE
A blockbuster miniseries.

Available at your favorite retail outlet.

HARLEQUIN®

Temptation

Look us up on-line at: http://www.romance.net   HTEHFH

COMING NEXT MONTH

#705 BODY LANGUAGE Margaret Brownley
Hero for Hire

Rick Westley was convinced the letter bomb that destroyed his office was a fluke. Who'd want to hurt *him*? But after spending a few days with Jacquie (Jack) Summers "protecting" him, he suspected someone *was* out to get him...and that someone was his sexy yet accident-prone bodyguard.

#706 THE ADVENTUROUS BRIDE Molly Liholm

Megan Cooper was surprised—and delighted—when sexy, rugged Adam Smith broke in to her bookstore and held her hostage. Before she knew it, he'd stolen her heart. Before *he* knew it, Meg was helping his investigation—and tempting him with her passion. Now Adam was the one in danger...of falling in love.

#707 TALL, DARK AND RECKLESS Lyn Ellis
Mail Order Men

Lone Star Lover? Texas Ranger Matt Travis thrived on taking risks, on encountering the unexpected—until he found himself corralled by a throng of sex-starved women! Worse, gorgeous TV newscaster Dee Cates seemed to be enjoying his predicament. And suddenly Matt was tempted to live up to his reputation....

#708 FLIRTING WITH DANGER Jamie Denton
Blaze

Tough cop Mason O'Neill figured he'd seen it all. Clearly gorgeous, sexy Bailey Grayson was out of her element on the streets of L.A. He arrested her to keep her safe. But who would protect Bailey from him...and his burning desire for her?
